It
WAS
YOU

RAED SLEWA

CONTENTS

1. The Promise 7

2. Survival Mode 13

3. Realization 19

4. True Death 27

5. The Hunger Vote 35

6. The Language of the Gods 44

7. Barbershop 57

8. Iraq TV 66

9. A Lady from the Past 75

10. The First Day of School 80

11. Hate and Religion 98

12. No Power. No Life. 116

13. The Second Separation 133

14. No Fear but Freedom 139

15. The Army of Illusions 153

16. Completion of the Soul 188

17. English Teacher 196

18. The Third and Fourth Separation 200

19. The Result: 99.96% 214

20. Harsh Letter 229

21. Goodbye for Now 232

22. Loneliness 245

Inspired by real events
and people

CHAPTER
One

The Promise

Fremont, California, 2017
Adam: 33 years old

I'm no longer living in Iraq. Instead, as I always wanted, I'm living in the United States, a lifelong dream finally realized, and I've been hired by one of the most respected automotive companies in Silicon Valley.

Yet, here I am, sitting by my apartment window, watching the dying, beautiful November leaves as they fall, debating whether the double-edged razorblade in my hand is sharp enough to set me as free as the leaves outside my window.

I press the blade to my wrist, and warm blood rushes onto my tan skin as I whisper to myself, "This is the least pain I've ever experienced."

My gaze flits out the window. *Maybe death is as beautiful as these dying leaves.*

There is only one way to find out.

My phone buzzes, and I jump—the razorblade slips from my fingers and falls to the floor. "Damn it. Why didn't I turn that thing off?"

Jon's name appears on my screen—a friend who never takes no for an answer.

I ignore the call, hoping he will delay his determination for a few minutes.

I pick up the razorblade and press it against my wrist. Harder this time.

Blood spills onto my jeans.

But my phone doesn't stop buzzing—the sound continues to interrupt my peaceful goodbye to this world.

Finally, I tell myself, *I'll have to answer him, or he'll never stop calling.*

"Hello," I say, my tone calm, unaffected, like my soul has already left my body.

"What the hell, man, why weren't you answering?" Jon yells at me.

I distance the phone from my ear and put him on speaker. Lifting the bottom of my white T-shirt to my wrist, I temporarily stop the bleeding, not caring if the stain ever goes away.

"I've been working long hours," I say. A lie. I skipped work for the past two days.

"Adam, please don't do it. I know you better than you know yourself. Don't shut down on me."

Jon *does* know me well. I usually don't give up, but when I do, everything that matters suddenly means nothing.

"What are you doing right now? Can you come back to Michigan? Your family and I need you. I want you to remember that." Jon's tone shifts, growing more worried as he adds, "I need you to remember the pain you feel won't go away if you end your life, you'll only be forcing it upon the people you love."

Does he have cameras in my apartment? I shake my head at the thought. "What makes you think I'm trying to end my life, Jon?"

"Adam, throughout the past 17 years, have I ever misread you?"

A few days ago, on the phone, I did tell him that everything around me felt useless. I told him that I'd forgotten why I was trying in the first place—to survive the war or the abuse. He must have become suspicious, especially because I hadn't answered his calls for the past two days.

I don't know how to answer him. I continue to apply pressure to my small wound with my white T-shirt, hoping our conversation will be over soon.

"You do recall what we went through in Iraq, right? Whatever you're going through right now, it can't possibly be the worst thing that's ever happened to you, *can* it?" Before I have a chance to respond, he continues, "Adam, promise me now." He waits several seconds. "Can you *hear* me?"

"Yes, I can hear you." My voice still sounds calm. The sycamore tree leaves are falling in large clumps now as the wind churns the air.

Jon repeats, "Adam, promise me."

My voice starts rising back to life. "Jon, how can I promise you something if I don't know what you're asking me?"

He responds quickly, "I want you to write down everything. From the beginning. Everything bad that's ever happened to you from our days in Iraq till now. I don't care if you write about your childhood, in fact, I *want* you to write about your childhood. We went through a hell of a lot of shit back in those days. And I don't care if what you write ends up as long as a novel, as long as you include all the details. I want to read everything."

Jon always dreamed of being a psychiatrist when we were in Iraq, and I hate being his subject today, but he cares about me, and he keeps me going, in his own way. I must hear him out.

"You were with me, Jon," I say. "Why the hell would you want me to write it?"

"No, I wasn't. I wasn't there for your *early* childhood. I only know bits and pieces of that story. C'mon, I promise this is the only request I'll ever ask of you, and then you're free to do whatever want, but I won't hang up the phone until you promise me." Jon's tone is desperate. He needs to hear me say the word "promise." He's aware, once he gets that word, he *knows* I'll deliver.

I laugh nervously. "You want me to write down everything?"

"Yes, everything," Jon answers without hesitation.

I pause for a few seconds. "And what, exactly, is the purpose of doing this?"

"I have my reasons, but they're my reasons. All you need to know is that I want this favor from you, and I won't hang up until you promise to deliver. And guess what? I have all day long for you, buddy."

My wrist is starting to ache, and I want him to

hang up. "Okay. I promise. But are you confident my writing won't get *you* depressed if it reminds you of our old lives?" I wait for a second and then add, "You may regret asking me to do this."

"Well, then," he says, laughing, "remind me to smile every now and then when I read what you write."

"I'll try," I say. "Talk to you later."

As I hang up the phone, the last sycamore tree leaf gives up its life and falls to the ground, refusing to wait for me. I whisper to myself, "Damn it. I'll need to patch my wound better than this, before I start fulfilling Jon's mad request."

CHAPTER
Two

Survival Mode

Baghdad, 1990
Adam: 6 years old

To: Jon
From: Adam
Subject: Here I go, fulfilling your mad request...

The booming sound that struck my room on the morning of January 17, 1991 wasn't the loud, scary 4 a.m. Muslim prayers they recited through the speaker of the mosque's towers for the whole city to hear and obey. This sound was different. This sound caused the ground to shake beneath me, sending all the pictures on my bedroom walls crashing to the floor. I opened my eyes, ready to cry and scream for my mom, but she was already there, snatching me from my bed. Then she grabbed my eight-year-old brother, Rami, and ran downstairs and outside toward the dark, black-painted, and isolated room in our backyard.

"Mom, please don't take us to the dark room," I pleaded with her, my face resting on the side of her sweaty forehead.

Rami had told me a monster lived in the dark room, that my dad kept him caged there. Of course, I believed every single word.

As we ran, I shouted, "No, Mama, there is a monster! Please, don't take us in there!"

She ignored my whining and continued running, outside our house and toward the dark room.

The night sky was filled with hundreds of beautiful red lights crossing from all sides, and it distracted me for a second. I couldn't take off my eyes off of them. But when I connected the red lights to the scary sounds, those lights taught me for the first time that beautiful things could also be terrifying.

As we approached, my dad opened the door to the monster's room from the inside. Since the loud sounds blocked all others, including his voice, he started waving his hands frantically, motioning for us to hurry up.

Another booming sound shook the ground beneath us. My mom stumbled, and the three of us fell into the backyard sand. My father sprinted toward us. Quickly, he tucked my mom under one of his arms and Rami and me under the other, and then he ran.

His wide arms could hold even more people, I thought to myself, clinging to him as he raced toward the dark room.

When we entered, I squeezed my eyelids closed, careful not to catch a glimpse of the monster. Maybe if I didn't see him, he wouldn't see me.

My sixteen-year-old sister, Rana, spoke first, "Mom is Adam bleeding?"

I cracked my eyes open for a second. My siblings were there. Rami: my eight-year-old brother who had been carried here with me. Reem: my ten-year-old sister who was probably as scared as the rest of us but didn't show it. Amar: my twelve-year-old brother who was standing in the corner by himself. Nabeel: my fourteen-year-old brother who had a book clutched in his hands. And Rana: my sixteen-year-old sister whose eyes were as large as saucers as she looked at my mom and me.

Rami, with his wild imagination, had lied to me. There was no sign of any monster. My family took up all the space in the tiny, 12-by-10-foot, dark room.

No monsters here. Just family.

Realizing the truth bought me a moment of relief, but soon after, the amount of the blood on my shirt took all my attention.

No one was sure if the blood was mine or my mom's or both, so my mom ignored the wound on her side and checked every inch of my body for injury. She found nothing. Only then, did she lift her own shirt to reveal a gash that my dad immediately covered with a cloth.

"Go check on the kids. I'll be fine," my mom told my dad, her heavy breathing interrupting her words for a moment before she added, "And make sure you turn off the lights, except for one candle."

My dad went to work, and my mom taped the cloth he'd given her to her side, before she rushed to start opening cardboard boxes full of clothes and toothpaste on the far end of the room.

"Rana help me out," my mom went on, handing out clothes to my sister in a hurry. "Don't forget the toothpaste, and make sure all your siblings' faces and necks are completely covered. It's happing tonight."

Rana had a calm, yet intense, expression on her face. Her black-as-night hair was pulled back into a ponytail that reached her shoulders, and she was ready to preform whatever task she was assigned.

I didn't understand much that night. As the bangs continued, I waited, not sure what to do, my eyes shifting around the room as I wondered what would happen next.

My mom took five sweaters and two tubes of toothpaste and rushed toward me. Because my shirt was covered in blood, it made sense that she wanted to exchange it for a clean item of clothing. But after my mom dressed me in the first sweater, on top of the bloody one, she continued dressing me in the others, and she didn't stop until a total of six sweaters covered my upper body.

"Stop it. What are you doing? I can't breathe," I told my mom, trying to push her away from me. With six sweaters on my body and all of us huddled in the dark room, the heat was sweltering. Even the winter weather of January in Baghdad couldn't beat the heat.

Rami tried to comfort me in his own way. "You'll need those sweaters, so the monster won't be able to eat you, Adam."

My mom interrupted him. "There are no monsters. How many times do I have to tell you? Stop putting those ideas in your brother's head!"

As she scolded Rami, she began smearing toothpaste all over my face, and I quit resisting. My face matched my siblings' now, and once my mom finished with me, she and my father dressed in sweaters and covered their faces with the toothpaste too.

"I hope the toothpaste and extra clothes are enough to save us from a chemical weapons attack," my dad said to mom while smearing his face with toothpaste, and then he took her hand, "But no matter what happens, we have to stick together."

"We must blow out the candle just as they announced on TV," my mom said as she pushed past Rami and Nabeel to get to the candle on a small, wooden table in the center of the room. "No light should be glowing from any house."

With a single breath, she blew out the candle as the last our strength dwindled.

As the night progressed, exhaustion claimed my strength, and I fell asleep, not understanding or knowing what had just happened.

Jon: I want you to smile. This was not the worst thing that ever happened to me.

CHAPTER
Three

Realization

Baghdad, 1990
Adam: six-years-old

As six-year-old boy, I did not understand what the word "war" meant. I expected my everyday life would go back to normal. Tomorrow, I would wake up in the morning and eat my favorite breakfast: Kahi, an Iraqi pastry with sugary syrup, and hot black tea with milk. After breakfast, I would chase the sand lizards in my backyard.

But for my family, life would never look the same again.

My parents were aware of what we would go through. They knew we needed to take extra precautions. We were a Christian family in a Muslim country that had no affirmative acceptance for other religions, so they were practiced at being careful.

The day after the first airstrike, I cracked my eyelids open, hoping I would no longer find myself in the darkroom. But there I was, cramped, on the floor with my three brothers, two sisters, and two parents—all eight of us lying on the floor of the 12-by-10-foot space, dried toothpaste on our faces making us appear like ghosts in the dark room.

Darkness reigned in the room, regardless of what time of day it was, with only a single window that my dad had covered in black vinyl paper.

"Mom, I want to go pee," I whined, hoping my excuse would award me temporary freedom.

My mom looked to my dad. "Is it safe now?"

"Well," my dad responded, glancing around the room. "Since no bombs are falling anymore, I would say, yes."

After my dad's assessment of the situation, my mom and I stepped outside, my mom carefully holding her wounded side with one hand, while she took my hand in the other.

Black smoke filled the sky, and the smell of burning tires overpowered my senses, almost as if black, hand-shaped tendrils of the foul-smelling smoke were reaching into my core and ripping out my soul.

I vomited into the sand.

My mom let go of her wound and held my head steady, stroking my forehead as she whispered in a soothing tone, "It's okay. It's okay." The words were a mantra for both me and her as a I threw up. "Shh. It's okay."

Because she held the power that moms do when you're only six, her words comforted me, and I believed it was going to be okay.

After I finished vomiting and after I peed, we went back into the dark room.

"Putrus, are you sure there was no chemical attack?" my mom asked my dad.

My dad held up the radio in his hands, attempting to tune it to different frequencies. "On the radio, they assured that."

My mom wasn't satisfied. "So, then, what's the burning smell?"

"American bombs," my oldest brother, Nabeel, replied solemnly before my dad could.

My dad's expression was grim. "Okay, next step, kids," he said, steering the conversation in a different direction. "I'm going to take a walk around the house and check if everything is safe before we all move back in." He motioned to Nabeel. "Nabeel, come with me."

They both walked outside.

After waiting patiently for fifteen minutes, my father shouted at us from the house's main door, "It is all clear, you can come on out now."

Even though everything did not appear okay or all clear, Rami flung the metal door of the dark room open, and we all nearly bowled over each other as we rushed toward the house.

My mom yelled after us, "Hey, easy! You'll trip and fall!"

We ignored the warning.

Rami slowed and looked around, wide-eyed. "What happened?"

"The war happened," Nabeel replied, his tone solemn. He had a flair for the dramatic, but in this case, his tone was appropriate. He went on, "The windows are broken, but the tape held everything in place."

"Shrewd move, Dad," Rana said. "Taping every-thing with duct tape was a good idea."

By the proud expression on my father's face, you would have thought he'd just single handedly stopped the war; instead, he saved our home from being destroyed. Not that it was a small feat. Taping the windows *had* been a clever idea.

Rami and I rushed upstairs to our room on the second floor. We were disappointed. The tape on our bedroom windows hadn't withstood the pressure, and broken glass was scattered all over our two beds.

"I'm glad Mom snatched me before our window spread into pieces all over my head," Rami told me.

"God saved us all last night," my mom said. She'd silently shadowed us up the stairs without us noticing.

Nabeel called out to everyone from the flat, second-story roof, "Come check this out! You're not going to believe it!"

We all rushed to the roof—the same roof we all slept on during the summers when the Baghdad heat became too stifling in the house—and saw Nabeel pointing at dozens of bullets, roughly 3 inches in size, lying on the floor of the roof, and others that had penetrated halfway through roof itself.

"These bullets missed their target," my twelve-year-old brother, Amar, commented.

The bullets were from Russian weapons used by the Iraqi military to shoot down American bombs.

"Unbelievable how we dodged all these bullets," my dad said, scratching the stubble on his face.

"God protected us. God protected us," my mom repeated to herself.

My dad looked into the distance and frowned, then he warned us, "We must go the safe room as soon the city siren starts. We cannot waste any time if there is another strike. We must be on alert at all times."

As my family continued to talk and clean up, I wandered back to my room by myself. My biggest concern was the blue robot toy with a broken head that I'd inherited from my older siblings, so I went to find it, searching under broken glass.

My feet were bare, and to this day, I still remember the pain as a shard of glass sliced through my delicate, six-year-old feet as easily as an Arabian, sharp sword cutting through flesh.

Rana walked in a few seconds later, as my blood began to spill all over the floor, and I remember her terrified expression just before I passed out.

When I woke up later, my dad was reprimanding my siblings for not watching me.

"We must move back to the darkroom every day at 5 p.m. for the next seven days," my dad told them, "even if there isn't another strike."

They all thought he was punishing them for what happened to me, and they all tried to rebel.

"What? Why? If there's no city siren, why do we have to?" Amar complained first.

Reem my ten-year-old sister, who was usually reserved, waved her arms in the air hysterically and shouted, "No. No. No. I can't take another night in a dark room, please, I would choke!"

"Enough!" My mom yelled, not willing to listen to any more protests. "It is not up to any of you. We're all going to listen to what your dad says. He's just trying to keep us safe!"

I was still lying on the floor, looking up at all of them.

Rami crouched down beside me, and whispered in my ear, "It's all because of you. If you hadn't been so stupid and stepped on the broken glass, we wouldn't have to go back to the dark room."

"Shut up. It's not my fault."

But it didn't matter whose fault it was.

Not just for the next seven days, but for the next

thirty days we followed our dad's plans. During the day we stayed in the house, but at night when the city siren roared and the loud noises began, when the red lights soared through the skies, we went back to the dark room. And for thirty days, we became accustomed to wearing sweaters, smearing toothpaste all over our faces, and smelling an odor like burning tires in the morning air.

After thirty days, the six-year-old version of myself, finally realized what the word "war" meant, even if it was just a glimmer.

Jon: I want you to smile. This was not the worst thing that ever happened to me.

CHAPTER
Four

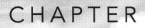

True Death

Baghdad,1990
Adam: six years old

After one month of airstrikes, we'd all managed to
survive.

Still, we were out of food, and we didn't have power.
Our water was now scheduled to run only five hours a
day, since the city water facilities had been hit bad, and
I wasn't sure if the money my dad had from his hard
work at the barbershop would be worth anything now.

My dad was already by the door, dressed and ready
to leave. "I'm going to go check the stores and see if
any of them are open."

"Okay. Don't go too far. We don't know how safe
it is," my mom said. Her worries were at their peak

during these days. Even though I was only a six-years-old, I could tell that she was on the verge of tears every time my dad or one of my siblings wanted to go out.

As usual, my oldest brother, Nabeel, joined our dad as he ventured away from our home, and Amar, my next oldest brother, went too.

There were no buses or Taxis in service at the time, so the only way to get around was to walk.

Two hours into their trip, we hadn't heard anything from them, and my mom started to panic, even though the stores were three miles away.

Rana tried to calm her down. "Let's not worry yet, mom. I'm sure the closest store was closed, and they're checking the others."

My mom's anxious expression didn't recede as she paced back and forth.

Our home phone line rang, startling us. Even without power, the phone was the one thing in our house that continued to operate.

My mom answered immediately. "It's your dad!" she shouted, a smile spreading across her face, but then her expression shifted, her brows furrowing as she said, "Salem?" She couldn't hide the surprise or confusion in her voice.

Uncle Salem, my dad's brother, would only call when someone in the family was sick or needed help. He never called just to check in. Never just to talk or ask us how we were doing.

"Is everything okay?" my mom asked.

We all waited as Uncle Salem responded on the other end of the line.

After a moment, my mom answered, "No, he's not home right now. He went to see if any of the stores are open. I can have him call you when he gets back."

A few more seconds passed. The crease between her eyebrows deepened. "You're coming here? Now? Did something happen?"

Salem must have abruptly hung up the phone, because my mom looked at the phone in puzzlement before she placed in back on the receiver.

Another two hours passed, and neither my father nor my siblings had showed up. By that point, my mom had nearly lost her mind with worry—talking to herself, whispering words we didn't understand. She'd practically worn a path in the floor from her non-stop pacing, and she'd forgotten all about Uncle Salem's weird call.

"I'm going after them," my mom finally said,

striding toward her room to get dressed, but then someone knocked loudly on the door.

My mom rushed to open the door, nearly falling backwards when it was Uncle Salem on our doorstep instead of my dad and brothers.

Uncle Salem looked disheveled. Dark circles were under his eyes, and he had a serious expression, like someone who'd just woken up from the grave. Behind him, stood two men in military uniforms holding a long, tan, wooden coffin. And behind them, was a military vehicle.

My mom lost her balance and fell to her knees. Her voice quivered as she asked, "Salem, what is this?"

My uncle held her arms, trying to help her up from the ground, but he still hesitated to answer.

"What's going on?" my mom screamed.

Salem looked over our mother's shoulders. "Take the kids upstairs," he said to Rana, addressing her like an adult, like she wasn't a kid herself, even though she was only sixteen.

Rana grabbed Reem and me and dragged us upstairs. The whole time she whispered to us "Whatever it is, we will be okay. We will be okay."

As we climbed the stairs, I heard Salem tell my

mom, "It's Mosa. He died in the recent airstrike. The army gave us what is left of him." Salem broke down, this time leaning on my mom for support. He shed no tears, but he sounded as if someone had amputated his arm as he wailed the words, "Mosa is dead! Mosa is dead! Mosa is dead!"

We rushed to Rana and Reem's room, but we could still hear Uncle Salem grief-stricken howling down-stairs until Rana shut the door.

She pulled out her ugly, old Barbie and gave it to me. "Here, Adam, you can play with this."

Silent tears slipped down Rana's cheeks as she stood there, motionless.

Reem went to her bed and put a pillow on top of her head, not willing to accept what she'd heard.

I glared at the miserable, old Barbie, and then I looked at Rana. I didn't understand why she was crying.

None of it made any sense to me, not when I was only six.

My Uncle Mosa was another one of my dad's broth-ers, and his wedding had taken place a few nights before the airstrikes had started. Maybe a week or two before. It was hard to keep track of time when the airstrikes had been going on for so long now.

Uncle Salem had said that Mosa was dead, but I didn't understand what the word "dead" meant.

I'd played the dead game with Rami before.

He'd tell me, "You're dead, Adam. Close your eyes and raise your right leg."

Whenever a player died in the game, he had to raise his leg, because it let the other players know that he was dead. But eventually, when the game was over, everyone that was dead woke up. I woke up.

"Mosa will wake up again, right?" I asked Rana. She only stared at me, so I kept talking, "We have to tell Mom. I always play this game with Rami. He'll wake up. There's no need to be upset. It's just a game. He'll wake up again soon."

My sister leaned towards me but didn't speak. Instead, she hugged me, then murmured, "No, it's not that type of death, Adam. He went to live with Jesus. We won't see him again any time soon."

"Why would he do such a thing? He wants to live in that old building we go to every Sunday?"

Rana didn't respond, only laid back on her bed.

My uncle Mosa was a twenty-one-year-old man, and by law, men had to join the Army at age eighteen—it was mandatory. Mosa would never have volunteered to be in the Army. And he never wanted to fight in any war, at least that's what I remembered my dad saying to my mom.

I remembered Uncle Mosa as a kind, happy, friendly person. He loved to throw me up in the air. And with him, I was never afraid of falling; instead, my laughter and joy filled the whole house. I trusted my kind uncle to catch me, and even though I didn't fully understand it at the time, his life had ended in the worst possible way.

"Why did they bring his body here?" Reem asked Rana.

Rana responded quietly, "Mosa and dad were close, and dad wouldn't forgive Salem or the rest of the family if they didn't give him the chance to say goodbye."

A few hours passed, and I began to feel hunger pangs in my stomach. Rana and I crept downstairs to eat.

The coffin rested on the floor, and my mom and Uncle Salem waited by the window for Dad to return.

The other two men in military uniforms, who'd come with my Uncle Salem, were gone.

The main door opened, and my dad and siblings entered.

My dad was smiling, thrilled to share the results of their trip. "Kids, we finally brought food!" he exclaimed. He turned towards my mom, waiting for her applause, but instead he saw my mom sitting still, tears tracking down her cheeks.

"What's wrong?" he asked and then added, "I'm sorry. I know I'm late."

She gestured with her head to the other side of the room, indicating the coffin with my Uncle Salem standing guard beside it.

My dad dropped the grocery bags, and food scattered all over the floor as he raised both hands to his head.

Amar and Nabeel froze in the background, two stone statues, their eyes unblinking. The relentless tick of the wall clock seemed to stop.

"Who is it?" my dad mumbled.

My mom went toward him, hugged him, and whispered, "It's Mosa."

Jon: I want you to smile. This was not the worst thing that ever happened to me.

CHAPTER
Five

The Hunger Vote

Baghdad, 1990
Adam: six years old

The war ended temporarily. For a few days, the airstrikes ceased, and I no longer saw red lights in the night sky.

During the airstrikes, our two local TV channels hadn't been broadcasting—the studios had been shut down and the news anchors had been sheltering in place like the rest of us. But with the temporary cease fire, power had been restored for a few hours each day, and the two local channels went back to airing from 2 p.m. until midnight.

They told us that the current government was still in power, and life would go back to the way it was before.

"Are you are going to open the barbershop, Putrus?" my mom asked my dad, looking up at him with wide, worried eyes.

My dad avoided her gaze. "Yes, what else can I do? We have to resume our regular life."

My mom didn't hold back her opinion on the matter, the words tumbling from her lips in quick succession. "Who's going to pay for a haircut when their kids might starve to death? Be realistic, Putrus! We're running out of food!"

I didn't agree with my mom's sentiment. Even though I was only six, I had strict standards when it came to my hair. I always wanted it to look as perfect as possible. After we'd gotten used to the war and the sound of the city siren blaring at night, I'd resumed putting effort into my appearance.

I would stand in front of Reem's mirror and inspect how well my dad had cut my hair and ponder how it could be improved. In addition, I started using my sister's hair oil to make sure my hair shined to perfection before we went to hide in the darkroom. Everyone in my family made fun of me for the odd practice, but it didn't stop me. I always made sure my hair was flawlessly combed, even on the worst days.

I told my mom, "Mom, I care about my hair."

My dad grinned. "Of course, you do." He lifted me from the ground and examined my shiny, medium-length, silky, sideways hairstyle. Then he set me on the ground and went on, "You tell your mom, Adam. Never be afraid of telling a woman what you think." He smiled again, looking over at my mom as he burst out laughing.

"God help us all," she said, rolling her eyes as she shook her head and walked away.

～

The next day my dad showed up with 100 kilograms of dark flour.

"Thank the Lord for his blessings," my mom murmured. Even the foul, dark-aged flour couldn't stop my mom from thanking God as usual, though she did raise another issue. "We're out of propane."

"I expected as much," my dad said, "and I thought we might use the oil heater for cooking and baking." His ability to find alternative solutions helped us through the worst of times.

My mom pursed her lips, thinking. "How long will it take to bake bread on top of the oil heater?"

"There's only one way to find out," my dad replied, heading to the storeroom to pull out the heater.

For weeks we sat around the small, handheld heater—in Iraq, we called it the Ala-eldean—watching my mom bake the dark-flour-bread for breakfast, lunch, and dinner.

It tasted so bad that I did everything I could not to eat it. I frequently skipped my meals. One day, I even skipped all three meals, because I found living worms sharing the flour with us.

"Mom, there are bugs inside my bread," I said, pointing out the little, brown worms squirming around in my bread. I hoped that informing her would stop her from baking the bread, but it didn't.

"I'll just pick them out," she said. "They're only harmless little bugs. But don't mention it to your siblings, please."

"Why not?"

"Because this is all we can afford to eat, and I don't want them to stop eating."

"I'll pick them out," she repeated, and then added hastily, "It's nothing. They're just harmless, little bugs searching for food too."

I didn't tell my siblings anything, but I couldn't get

over the bug image in my head, and I refused to eat.

Eventually, my mom forced me to eat every time I resisted, and in time, the hunger pains in my belly helped my mom break me of my stubbornness.

After a few weeks on dark-flour-bread, the lack of nutrition affected us all. I could count all of my ribs, and my hipbones jutted out. I had none of the energy of a normal six-year-old boy, and I remember hours spent laying by the Ala-eldean, hours spent trying to regain my energy and get warm.

While I was laying down by the Ala-eldean my oldest brother, Nabeel, started questioning my dad about how long this would last. My father promised he'd figure it out. But Nabeel wouldn't relent, and eventually, my father yelled at him in frustration and went outside.

"Can I join you?" Nabeel asked him.

"No, take care of your brothers!" Dad yelled back.

Nabeel kicked a chair in frustration, and Amar approached him with a question. "What would happen if we ran out of food?"

Nabeel responded immediately without thinking, "Hmm, I'm not sure. Maybe we would start eating our youngest siblings instead of taking care of them!" He stomped out of the room.

Amar glanced over at me with an evil smile and said, "Be ready, Adam, in case we decide to chop and fry you on top of the Ala-eldean." Then he followed Nabeel out of the room.

I didn't know if they were serious, so I gathered what little strength I had and ran upstairs to talk to Rana.

"Are you okay? What's wrong?" Rana asked.

"Is it true?"

"Is what true?"

I hesitated. I didn't want to tell her what they'd said, because I didn't want to give her any ideas. What if she started thinking about eating me too?

So, I stood there and cried.

Rana hugged me. "Who hurt you? I'll kick their ass!"

Rana could take down any of my siblings if she wanted to.

"Nabeel and Amar said they would chop and fry me once we ran out of food, is it true?"

She smirked and replied, "Those idiots!" She bent down and took my hands in hers. "Do you trust me, Adam?"

I nodded, but I wasn't really sure what that word meant.

"I promise I won't let anyone hurt you."

I understood her promise well enough, and I decided to stay in her room, so I could feel the power of her protection.

A few hours later, a loud noise came from the living room downstairs, claiming our attention. When we went downstairs to check it out, we found the family huddled around the TV with the volume set to max.

"Jesus, who's deaf here?" Rana commented, but no one replied to her.

The war songs of Saddam Hussein blasted from the screen, followed by videos of him waving to enormous, cheering crowds. My family, however, was solemn. They never expressed any happiness when he appeared on TV.

Nabeel asked, "So they will announce it today?"

My father was sitting in a chair placed a few feet away from the TV, his expression sober, but he turned around to answer Nabeel. "Yes, they will announce it today. I truly hope they vote to wave the war sanction and that everything goes back to normal."

I tried to put together my family's puzzling conversation, and after sitting in the living room for about an hour, I'd gathered that some people somewhere would vote to determine whether we would be allowed to have food or not. It didn't make sense to me why these people would not let us eat. What would they gain from starving our family? And even worse, I could end up on top of Ala-eldeen as a meal!

I wanted so badly for everything to be normal.

I wanted to eat my favorite cake that Mom used to bake, and I wanted warm Kahi for breakfast. I wanted to eat Mom's delicious Dolma—meat and rice stuffed grape leaves—for lunch and maybe some Biryani for dinner.

My mood improved, thinking about the meals.

"We can eat how we did before?" I asked Rana.

She turned towards me and smiled. "It's possible. You never know. Maybe we'll be able to eat the ice cream from the Ajrass store again."

The United Nations Security Council were having a vote that day to decide whether or not they were in favor of a sanction to cut off all financial support for Iraq via a full trade embargo, which meant, for most of Iraqi families, the struggle to find food at the market would continue because Iraq depended on imported goods.

With everyone in my family waiting around the TV, hoping the vote would result in forgiveness of

Iraqi war crimes in Kuwait, the news anchor finally appeared on the screen and started the announcement.

"Dear viewers," the news anchor said. "Sadly, the United Nations failed to deliver a fair judgment of the Iraqi government and Iraqi people."

My family's faces fell, but their eyes were still locked on the TV screen. I locked my eyes on the TV, trying to figure out whether or not these people were going to let me eat, but judging by my family's reaction, the news wasn't what they'd hoped.

Our dream of things to returning to normal was shattered.

No more imported goods would be allowed to enter Iraqi soil. My family would be relegated to eating the worm-filled, dark-flour-bread for an indefinite period of time.

To me, this was a hunger vote, and they'd all agreed to let us starve. My visible ribs and protruding hip bones wouldn't disappear any time soon.

Jon: I want you to smile. This was not the worst thing that ever happened to me.

CHAPTER
Six

The Language of the Gods

Baghdad, 1991
Adam: seven years old

After the hunger vote was passed to punish the Iraqi government for the Kuwait invasion, Saddam Hussein decided to challenge the rest of the world by starting a country-wide push to rely on local sources of food and other goods. He achieved his goal and provided free monthly food assistance for every family. Based on the number of people in a household, families received varying amounts of rice, cooking oils, flour, salt, lentils, and soaps. Though my skeletal image remained, things started to improve, and at least we had something to eat other than dark-flour-bread. Now, we had enough to keep us alive. Saddam

Hussein was hailed as the hero who'd saved Iraq from starvation. It didn't matter that he'd been the one to start the war in the first place.

With life stating to return to normal, the markets began opening up, selling locally sourced food and other goods. Then it was the schools.

Our local school, the same one my siblings had been attending for years, announced it would be opening its doors for students to return soon, and that meant I would be headed to school for the first time.

The next day my dad took me to our local school to register as a new student. My dad spoke with the lady at the registration desk in a different language than the one we spoke at home. The words sounded similar to the words I'd heard on TV in the war songs and the words I'd heard spoken by the TV reporters, but it sounded different when my dad and the lady spoke. I didn't understand the majority of what they were saying.

In the past, I'd only ventured outside my house when I had a doctor's appointment or when we'd visited relatives or when my dad had taken me to his barber shop and the Ajrass ice cream shop next door, but other than on those special occasions, I hadn't been allowed to go beyond our backyard wall.

Living with an overprotective family, made things hard for me. My parents would always tell me that young kids like me shouldn't wander or play outside alone. The same rules applied to my other young siblings.

"There are crazy and dangerous people outside the wall," my mom would say.

Kids often shouted in a language I didn't understand beyond the wall, so I'd believed my parents. People on the streets were crazy, and I was better off staying at home.

Once my dad and I arrived home from the school, I rushed to my mom and asked her, "Mom, did you know that dad speaks the crazy, weird language too?"

She laughed at me and replied, "You will learn to speak the same language, my eastern prince! They call the language Arabic, and it is the language you will be speaking in school and in public for all the years to come."

I looked up at her with wide, innocent eyes. "Why don't they speak how we do?"

She kissed my forehead and said, "My love, we are Christians! We speak Aramaic, the language Jesus himself once spoke! However, since we are a smart and blessed people, we are capable of speaking Arabic too. In fact, any language you want to speak, you can! All you need to do is to listen when people talk, and eventually, you will learn."

"Why don't they speak Jesus's language?" I asked my mom.

She replied, "Because Aramaic is a Chaldean language."

My family were Chaldeans, which meant we were Christians who spoke the Aramaic language. And Aramaic was utterly different than Arabic. When I was seven and starting school, only somewhere between 500,000 to 850,000 people spoke Aramaic worldwide.

At the time, I didn't fully comprehend who that Jesus guy was, nor did I fully comprehend why I should be so proud to speak His language. What good was His language if I couldn't communicate with anyone outside my house? The idea of not being able to communicate with most other people in Iraq terrified me.

Once I left my house for any reason, I became weak, vulnerable, and unable to say what I wanted.

When Rana and I went to the store, I couldn't

communicate with Abu-Hayder, the store owner. Without Rana, I would have been thrown out, because I couldn't communicate my desire to buy the store's locally-made, sugar-free popsicle.

I tried to communicate nonverbally by pointing to the freezer, but Abu-Hayder didn't understand what I wanted. With an annoyed expression, he gestured for me to get me out of his store. I started to leave, but Rana interfered.

"He is with me Abu-Hayder," she said. I understood some of her Arabic. For some reason, her words were clearer to me.

"So, what's wrong? He is old enough to speak, right?" Abu-Hayder said, still annoyed.

"You don't worry about it. My brother pointed at the popsicle, so give him what he wants." For a moment, Rana, with her tough talk, made me believe she owned every inch of the store.

We bought the popsicle and some other stuff my mom wanted, and I left the store hopeless and embarrassed.

Rana held my hand as we crossed the road. "Don't worry," she told me. "One day you will speak their language. You're so smart you will speak any language you want—many languages!" She tightened her grip. "I promise. You'll do anything you want." Suddenly, my bold sister had transformed into an angel of kindness.

The tears in my eyes were threatening to spill down my cheeks, but her words calmed me and gave me confidence.

Rana was a kind and soft-spoken person, but she morphed into a tough woman, who could tame a lion with a single look, when it is necessary. Her strength always inspired me to fight back, regardless of the circumstances.

Her spell had worked on me. I started paying extra attention to TV shows and listened. Words started making more sense. Eventually, I understood what the cartoon characters were saying.

I started singing the cartoon intro in Arabic the way I'd learned it on TV.

Rami broke out laughing. "That is the weirdest accent I ever heard." Unable to stop laughing, he shouted up the stairs, "Nabeel, Amar, come here. Come listen to Adam singing the Oskar cartoon intro."

Having decided to adopt Rana's strength and her robust personality, I channeled my inner self and didn't give up. In fact, I didn't hesitate to sing the song again and again.

"Your accent reminds me of Grandfather," Amar said, laughing.

"Repeat the first section again," Nabeel requested, practically giggling.

"Did he say penis instead of—"

I cut off Rami before he finished. "At least my accent is more interesting than your boring street accent. Everyone has it, so what makes you so special?" I held my head high and strolled out of the room singing.

School would start in two weeks, and I still wasn't completely confident about it. How would I communicate if I couldn't manage to buy a sugar-free popsicle by myself? How would I go to school and talk to all the other kids and the teachers? But Rana's words rose in my mind again. I couldn't give up. I didn't want people to treat me the way Abu-Hayder had.

In Iraq, people would taunt anyone who didn't speak Arabic fluently. My grandfather used to get mocked for his thick accent all the time.

My young body didn't allow me to crush their mean faces or break their ugly yellow teeth, but even if I had been able to do those things, my parents would never have approved of my actions.

They would tell me, "This is not about your grandfather or you. This is about them. Don't take it personally."

～

"It's time for you to come to work with me," my father told me one day as he fixed his dark hair while looking into the decorative mirror we had in the hallway. "School will start soon, and you must interact with people to learn the language."

"Can I start today?" I asked my dad.

"That's not a bad idea," my mom responded, passing us on her way to the kitchen.

"Okay," my dad said. "Go and change quickly. The first rule you must follow is to be on time. I can't be late, so you must always be ready to leave by 8:30 am, that way we'll be there before work starts at 9:00."

I was excited and curious about going to work with my dad. His shop was right next to the Ajrass store, where they sold the most delicious chocolate and vanilla ice cream I'd ever tasted.

So, when I got the go ahead from Dad, I didn't

hesitate to run upstairs and pull on the ripped, old jeans and worn out shoes I'd inherited from Rami. The shoes were at least two sizes too big for my tiny feet and the jeans didn't make me look my best, but I went to the bathroom and made sure my dark hair was combed perfectly anyway. I was sure my dad wouldn't approve of me setting foot in his barbershop if my hair was messy.

"I'm ready," I announced to my dad as I ran down the stairs.

"Perfect, let's go, my wolf."

At 8:30 am, we stepped outside the house, and I held my dad's hand proudly.

"So, do tell me, Adam, can you read any of these store signs," he asked as we passed a variety of local businesses and shops.

"No, I cannot read any, tell me what they say."

He smiled and started telling me about every shop on the street. He told me what each business did and told me what each shop sold. He told me the name of every shopkeeper too, and whenever we passed by someone on the street, he greeted them, as I proudly held his hand.

My father never took the bus to work. Since his

shop was only a little over a mile away from our
house, he would walk to work every day to save
money. But as we got closer to the shop, I started
plotting how I was going to convince my dad to buy
me the expensive ice cream from the Ajrass store next
door.

When we got there, though, I was devastated. The
Ajrass store windows had been shattered, and the
whole place had been caged with rusty metal bars and
chained with locks. The loud noises and the red lights
had claimed this place. It was no longer the happy
store it had once been, the store with long lines of
cheerful kids waiting for ice cream. It had been utterly
destroyed.

"No!" I stopped suddenly, forcing my dad to stop
too.

My father turned towards me, surprised. "What's
wrong?" he asked. He looked at me for a second, and
then followed my grief-stricken gaze to the Ajrass
store. "Oh, yes. It's terrible, isn't it? Abu-Mohanad
should have listened to me and tapped his windows,
but more importantly, he shouldn't have stayed late
to make extra ice cream cones. He wanted an extra
buck, and it cost him his life. He died in there, along

with his oldest son. They pulled them out five days after the strikes ended."

Even to this day, I didn't know why he delivered the news to me like I was an adult. Maybe he thought I deserved the truth after all I'd been through, but I couldn't accept the fact Abu-Mohanad had died, and even worse, his cheerful son Mohanad had too! Because my Uncle Mosa had died, I now understood what the word "dead" meant, and I knew that I would never see the shopkeeper or his son again.

"So, that's it? They're gone? No more ice cream?" I asked the questions as if they all held the same weight.

My father responded, "Yes, that's it. They're gone, son, and as of right now, no ice cream shops are being allowed to open anyway because of the government's new rules regarding sugar. The sugar-free popsicles are all that's allowed, and anything that requires a lot of sugar is banned."

In the years following the full trade embargo, the Iraqi government banned all products that required a significant amount of sugar. The goal was to avoid a sugar shortage and to keep the cost of local sugar down.

My dad had delivered the bad news to a

seven-year-old boy bluntly, and I stood there, shocked.

My dad said, "Let's go." He gripped my hand and nearly dragged me to his shop. "Listen to me, son. In life, you must be prepared to lose everyone and every-thing at any time. Otherwise, you will always be sad and shocked."

We continued walking to the shop, and I said nothing.

My dad didn't want me to be too attached to anyone. If my own happiness were dependent upon other people or things, he believed it would only hurt me. Nothing was forever, and he wanted to make sure I was prepared to accept the loss of everything and everyone that I loved most, wanted to make sure I was prepared for the possibility of sudden disappearances.

What about Mom and Rana and all my siblings? I asked myself.

I would never be ready to lose them, not on any day or at any hour. I would never be ready to lose their smiles or their unconditional love.

They were not just people to me; they were each part of my soul.

I didn't approve of my dad's advice, but what he'd

said about nothing being forever was the truth, and the words stayed with me, adding to the fear I carried inside.

Jon: I want you to smile. This was not the worst thing that ever happened to me.

CHAPTER
Seven

Barbershop

Baghdad, 1991
Adam: seven years old

My parents decided I would go to work with my
dad until school started. We worked from 9 a.m.
to noon, and then again from 3 p.m. to 9 p.m. We
would normally go home in the middle of the day for
a three-hour break. Thinking about it now makes me
smile—what a funny schedule! But my dad owned the
shop, so he was able to work any schedule he wanted.

Working with Dad didn't bother me at first; however, when he started asking me to remove used barber
capes covered in hair from the customers shoulders,
I wasn't pleased. As I removed the capes, I had to
tell the customers, "Naimaa amo," which meant,

Blessings upon you, sir, and I hated how tiny bits of hair would fly all over my clothes and face.

I didn't want to do it again, so I ignored a customer.

My dad yelled at me, "What did I tell you to do?"

"Dad, I didn't want to touch him. There is hair everywhere, and it's disgusting. Plus, the guy smelled."

My father shouted at me again, and at this point, I was refusing to anything he said, when another customer walked in.

"Alsalamo alekom," the customer greeted us in Arabic. *Peace be upon you.*

I didn't know how to answer in Arabic. So, I stared at him and wondered if he was clean enough for me to remove the barber cape once he was done.

My father responded, "Wa alaekom Alsalam, Mr. Ali." *How are you?*

Ali replied, "Outstanding, and you? What is the shouting for?"

My dad smiled, transforming into a different person. When he answered his tone was calm, "Kids, Ali, you know how they are."

Ali replied with a deep voice and kind smile, "Yea, yea. They will learn. That's why they have us."

My father covered Ali with the brown, silk barber's

cape and began trimming his hair with sharp, silver scissors and a bright red comb.

The sound of the scissors—click, click, click—started as my dad told his usual stories about the war and people. Every click was separated by a precise number of seconds, and my dad's fingers danced along Ali's hair until it had transformed into a whole new style.

My father and Ali exchanged several stories in Arabic, and I barely understood them.

After about twenty minutes, my father brushed the loose hairs from Ali's neck, and he gestured with his head to remind me of my task.

I stood up, walked toward the chair, and took the barber cape in my hands. I lifted it from Mr. Ali's chest, and with a shy, scared, quiet voice, I said, "Naimma amo!"

I hoped my dad and Ali had heard what I'd said, so my dad wouldn't yell at me.

Ali peered over at me, kindness in his eyes and in his smile. My head translated his expression for me. When I looked at him, I saw love and a desire to protect me from harm. I recognized the quality in him, because it was the same one I saw in my mom and Rana's smiles.

Though my words had been barely audible, Ali said, "Good work. I appreciate you!" Then, he turned to my dad and said, "What a respectful son you have, Putrus!"

Ali's enthusiastic tone made it seem like he wanted to make sure my dad wouldn't have any negative criticisms of me after he left.

After paying my dad for the haircut, Ali took a few steps toward me and handed me twenty-five dinar. "Thank you! I didn't get your name."

My voice was a bit more confident now. "My name is Adam."

"Lovely name, Adam. Do you know what it means?"

In Arabic every name had a meaning, but I didn't know what my name's meaning was at the time.

I shook my head, so I wouldn't have to speak to him with my weird accent.

"Your name is so exceptional that it has three meanings. The first is the astronaut."

I understood the word "astronaut," because I'd learned it from an astronaut cartoon character. Mr. Ali owned all my attention.

"The second meaning is professional," he went on. "And the third is the greatest of them all. It is a person who will lead his people to treasures, knowledge, and peace. One day, Adam, you could fulfill all three of these meanings, but which one would you like to fulfill the most?"

"I would like to lead my people to treasure, knowledge, and peace."

He grinned at me. "Then, one day, that's what you will do." Turning to my dad, he said, "Maa elsalama." *Be safe.*

My father replied with the same expression.

My wide eyes followed Mr. Ali as he walked away, a small smile on my face. I'd achieved my first good experience communicating with someone beyond the walls of my house, and it was the complete opposite of the bad experience I'd had with Abu-Hayder.

My parents had been right. The barbershop, and the language exposure it provided, was my family's version of preschool. It gave me a chance to interact with people before school started.

My father began cleaning up and said, "Hand me the broom, Adam."

I gave him the heavy broom.

My father continued, "It wasn't so bad, right? You earned money today."

He had a smile on his face as he swept up, but
I ignored him as I peered out the window, hoping
another entertaining customer like Mr. Ali would
come in next.

The windows of the shop were still crisscrossed with
black duct tape, the tape my dad had put up before
the strikes, but I noticed one of the three windows had
been cracked. And now, duct tape was all that held
that window together.

"Bab," I said, pointing at the windows. *Dad.*

"Yes, I'm aware I'll have to take off the tape."

"No!" I practically shouted. "The window!" I
pointed to the crack.

He walked close to the one I pointed out. "Oh
Lord, I can't afford this now. Okay, stay away from
it, Adam." He made a phone call to the handyman
who used to fix anything that was broken around
the barbershop. "Damn it," my dad said after several
seconds. "He's not answering. Okay, let's put a cardboard box in front of both sides of the window, so
people won't lean over them until I take care of it."

We did, and by noon, we were headed back home
for our break. As we passed the Ajrass store, I was
once again reminded of wartime and death.

Further along our route home, we stopped by the fruits and vegetable store.

"Good afternoon," my dad said to the grocery guy who's untrimmed beard covered half his face and who's bushy eyebrows took up the other half, "let me have eight apples, please."

After the guy had put all the eight apples on the scale, he loaded them in the plastic bag and announced, "That'll be seven hundred and fifty dinars."

Buying fruit was so expensive that my dad had to get at least six to seven customers during the morning shift to afford it.

My dad reached into his wallet, and his cheeks turned red. With a nervous smile, he asked the guy, "Would you please take off two apples? Take off the big ones if you don't mind."

With an annoyed expression the guy took off the two apples and placed the bag on the scale again. "Five hundred and sixty-four dinars."

My father cleaned out his wallet and gave the guy all the money he had earned working in the barbershop that morning. My dad caught me staring at his empty wallet, and I could tell it made him uncomfortable. I quickly shifted my gaze away, thinking about how there were eight people in my family and only six apples. My parents would not eat any fruit.

We bought the apples, and we left the store, but after about twenty steps, I couldn't bear the thought of my parents not getting to have any fruit, so I ran back to the store and handed the clerk my twenty-five dinars. In broken Arabic, I said, "Give me two more apples, please."

He glared at me and said, "You cannot buy shit with this, boy, not even a real candy!"

His unnecessary anger helped me understand his words.

"Are you deaf, boy, get out!" the guy yelled rudely.

"Adam!" My father called my name in shock. "What are you are doing?" My father apologized to the guy, and we walked out. "Why did you do this?"

I responded in Aramaic. "I haven't gone to school yet, Dad, but I can tell we are missing two apples."

My father's lips tightened, and his expression grew sad. But he didn't say anything.

I was determined to make sure my mom and dad got to eat. So, I told him, "I don't like eating apples anyway." A lie. I loved apples. I continued, "You and Mom can cut one in half. I'm sure I will make more money from customers tonight, and I will buy popsicle from Abu-Hayder instead."

Though I had hoped to make my dad feel better, I didn't succeed. My father's face saddened further. He turned toward me, picked me up, and kissed me. But he couldn't hold his tears back any longer. They fell slowly down his olive-colored, clean-shaven cheeks.

My father whispered, "Mr. Ali was wrong when he said you might be the person who will lead his people to treasure, because you are the treasure itself, son."

He kissed me again as he carried me, and I hugged him, wrapping my tiny arms around his neck. I spent the rest of the walk home, in my dad's arms, hoping I could buy my dad as many apples as he wished one day.

Jon: I want you to smile. This was not the worst thing that ever happened to me.

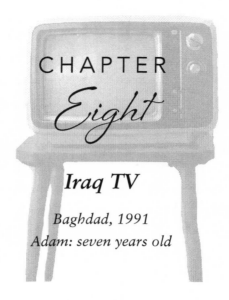

CHAPTER
Eight

Iraq TV

Baghdad, 1991
Adam: seven years old

When we finally arrived home, my father put me down, and we walked into the living room. All my siblings were lying down on the floor, facing the TV, but no shows had started airing yet, only a stupid picture of rainbow stripes.

As soon as my dad stepped into the room, they all jumped up, dashing for the bag of apples, making sure to claim theirs before someone could cheat and take two instead of one. Afterward, they ambled back to the living room and took up their assigned spots in front of the TV.

Everyone who lived in Iraq at the time had two TV

channels. The first channel specialized in telling world news, providing information about the war, and regaling Iraqi citizens with stories of Saddam Hussein's achievement. The second channel also broadcast the news, but they added a thirty-minute cartoon and a movie every night, which made the channel popular with youth and kids. The TV channel was even called Al-Shabab—*Youth.*

Al-Shabab started at 1 p.m., and my siblings were waiting impatiently for the channel to begin airing.

At 1:05 p.m., the rainbow stripes were still on, and Rami started complaining, "Come on, why is this shit not starting?"

From the other side of the room, my mom shouted, "Hey, watch your language! One more bad word, and the TV will be off all day." She meant what she said. She'd done it before with Amar.

Suddenly, the rainbow screen morphed into the flag of Iraq, and the Iraqi anthem began. After few minutes, a young girl in her early twenties with long, blond hair laying over her right shoulder appeared on the screen. To me, she seemed like the happiest person I'd seen on TV since the airstrikes.

She started the introductions with a clear,

straightforward tone. "Dear viewers, good afternoon. We're glad you're here with us, and we hope you'll enjoy our programs. First, we would love to start today's programming with a recitation from the Quran. Have a blessed day."

She disappeared from the screen, and many words—as if from a book—replaced the attractive, young girl. A man recited the words with a harsh tone, but I understood it.

Rami couldn't curse, not after my mom's warning. So, he said loudly, "Ahooo." It wasn't exactly as curse word, but we used it to convey annoyance and disagreement.

My mom scolded Rami, "Don't be disrespectful. This is also a religion, and you must respect it."

Rami mumbled, "I don't care. It's annoying."

Nabeel, my oldest brother, nodded. "I am Christian. I don't care what this guy has to say."

I couldn't stand the annoying voice on the TV, so I walked to the kitchen and asked my mom when she was planning to serve our lunch.

"In a few minutes," she said.

By the time we'd finished eating, the man on the TV had finished reciting the Quran.

Another lady came onto the screen and introduced the next program. This woman appeared more serious than the previous, younger girl, though she started her introduction with the same words.

"Dear viewers, good afternoon. We're glad you're here with us. From the family of Al-Shabab, we hope you will enjoy our programs. Our second program is called, *So We Don't Forget.* It's critical that we remember, every day, all of our loved ones who gave their lives for us in the war, and critical that we recognize these heroes who saved us from our evil enemy."

She disappeared from the screen, and then they began airing war, victory songs.

At this point, Rami lost it and started behaving hysterically. "No! This is stupid! Where is the cartoon?"

Amar yelled at him. "Shut up! They will show it after. Do I have to remind you every day?"

Rami ignored Amar.

On TV, they were showing a video of Saddam Hussein waving at people in his military uniform. People around him were singing and cheering happily. As they continued singing, I realized I understood some of the words.

"*You the father of the two lions Oday and Qusay.*

You are the light of our vision, and we are all yours. The sea itself gets thirsty, and from you, the sea drinks his water."

My mind immediately stopped and refused to translate any more words. How could those lyrics be correct?

I asked Nabeel in Aramaic, "Is that what those words mean or is my translation wrong?"

Nabeel laughed—could not stop laughing. "You're correct, Adam. That's what they mean."

While my mom picked up our dishes from lunch, she caught us in the middle of our conversation.

"Nabeel, Adam! Are you out of your minds? I don't want to hear such comments again. The walls have ears. Are you aware of what they do to people who make fun of these songs or Saddam Hussein?"

Nabeel and I did not respond and listened as she went on, "They pull their teeth out one-by-one and bury them alive." She pointed her finger at Nabeel. "You remember Adel?"

Nabeel's eyes widened and his face went white.

Our mom scolded him, "*Exactly.* I don't want you to start anything that could lead us all to our deaths, you understand?" Before Nabeel could say anything in response, my mom turned to me and said, "Moreover, you Adam, in a week or two, are going to school. Teachers may ask if you and your family approve of Saddam Hussein or if your family has an opinion about him that you can share. Don't you dare mention Nabeel's behavior today. You will have one answer. We love our leader and obey his wise decisions."

This conversation sounded crazier than the conversation I'd had with Rami about the monster in the darkroom. But everything my mom said was nothing but the truth. We would be killed, all of us, if they found out we made jokes about Saddam Hussein.

The conversation ended with me saying, "Yes, Mom. I will do what you said."

We continued watching TV, and I shut off my mind, stopping myself from translating any more of words in the ridiculous songs, hoping the song portion of the program would finish soon. It finally ended, and the title appeared again. *So We Don't Forget.* Whatever was coming next, that title didn't make it sound any better than the songs.

They showed images of a burnt child and mother holding each other.

"Wow, did they burn alive?" Nabeel asked.

The mother and child were in the Malja Al-Amareya, a building people would go to for shelter. During the earlier Iran-Iraq war, people use to go there to take shelter from falling rockets. It was considered a safe place, but apparently, it hadn't held up well this time.

They showed more pictures of burned bodies, wrecked buildings, and people's bloody body parts lying all over. They pulled a living child from a destroyed house, and his face was covered in blood and dirt—beside him, was a dead woman.

My heart shivered. *Where is my mom? I am sure she wouldn't approve of us watching this madness.*

She was walking back and forth between the living room and the kitchen, not paying attention to what we were watching. I said nothing. The four of us boys had remained in the living room. Nabeel, Amar, Rami, and I. My two sisters had given up after the first program, when they'd aired the Quran readings.

Or were they aware of what would come after? I questioned myself.

The videos and images of dead people didn't stop for fifteen minutes. It gave me a headache and a false sense of my surroundings, to such a degree that my eyes started shutting down. But I fought back against my blurring vision. My uncle Mosa was the only dead person I'd ever seen. Not anymore.

Another deep voice started talking toward the end of the program. "So we never forget how heartless our enemy is toward humanity."

Saddam Hussein appeared then, holding the hands of poor people on the streets, hugging them as if they were his sons Oday or Qusay. He waved at the people as they cheered and shouted, "With our soul, with our blood, we sacrifice for you!" The crowds repeated the words over and over.

The war ended on February 28, 1991, after the Iraqi army retreated from Kuwait. Regardless of the reality, on TV, they delivered lies and said that Iraq had won the war, calling the war, "Am Almaarek." *The mother of wars.*

They showed Saddam Hussein receiving several medals with a proud smile on his face, and then the video switched to the streets of Baghdad, showing how the government had rebuilt the wrecked buildings and how life had gone back to normal.

"The victory of 'Am Almaarek' is the most

magnificent achievement of our great leader Saddam Hussein," the same male voice said.

I told myself no one deserved a medal if innocent people died.

Finally, another introduction from the TV started, and they announced the time for the cartoon. My mind had shut off. I'd lost my desire to watch anything. How could I when I'd just seen the bodies of people burned alive? How could I watch anything after they'd broadcast lies about Iraq being the winner of the war? Iraq had lost the war. Everyone knew it. Even me, a seven-year-old boy. Yet the government forced the media to lie to the people and say otherwise.

Jon: This was not the worst thing that ever happened to me, but it was nearly the worst thing I've ever seen.

CHAPTER
Nine

A Lady from the Past

Baghdad, 1991
Adam: seven years old

My siblings were gathered around my mom saying,
"Let me see, mom. Let me see!"

I rushed to find out what they were trying to see.

"What is it?" I asked, but no one paid any attention
to my question. "What is it? What is it?"

Every time I asked the question, my voice rose louder
and louder, until I'd at least claimed Rami's attention.

"It's Lena," he said. "She sent a picture of her
newborn."

"Who's Lena?" I asked.

Rami looked at me with a weird expression. "I
don't have time for your silly humor." He reached

out for the pictures. "Oh, wow, her son has our nose, Mom."

I took one of the pictures to figure out who this lady was. She was a tall, young lady with dark hair and tan skin, and she carried a baby boy who looked identical to my own baby pictures. It didn't make any sense. Confused, I stared at the pictures.

Nabeel noticed. He said, "Mom, Adam doesn't know who Lena is, does he?"

My mom's brows drew together. "I don't think so." She looked at me. "You don't remember her, do you?"

I shook my head.

"When Lena left you, she cried hysterically. She told me that you were the one it would be hardest to leave." My mom's face saddened.

"Who *is* Lena?" I asked again.

"She's your sister!" my mom practically shouted.

"No, I can't remember Lena. Have you ever mentioned her name to me?"

My mom paused for a minute, her brows pulling together. "So much has been going on lately. I don't know if I have spoken with you about her. Well, it's time to tell you since you are old enough now, but you must keep this a secret."

"What do you mean?"

"Lena lives in America," my mom said. "We don't want any of our neighbors or friends to find out. We need to avoid any questions form the government. Do you understand? You are seven years old. You should be able to keep this as a secret now, okay?"

After I viewed and examined the picture a few more times, I did my best to remember. "This young lady used to carry me on her back and run around our backyard," I told my mom. "It's coming back to me. I *do* remember her."

My mom smiled. "You always cried whenever she left your sight." My mom laughed and added, "She couldn't even take a shower because you would cry so much when she left you."

"Why did she leave?"

"Before the war, she met her church friend's cousin when he visited from the United States. He fell in love with her, and they got engaged."

I glanced again at the picture while my mom recited the story.

There was a silver lining to Lena's story, even though I didn't know it at the time. My oldest sister, who I hardly remembered, was the hope for our future.

The picture was still in my head, even after all the pictures had been put away. Lena carried my nephew, and in the background, there were bright green trees, and there was bright green grass and a Cape Cod style house like the ones I'd only ever seen in the movies or on TV. Before seeing those pictures, I wasn't sure if those houses or places were even real.

I asked my mom if we could move to America.

"I wish, son, but there is no way for us to travel, especially to a country we are at war with. You can't tell anyone where Lena lives. We told everyone she lives in Jordan."

I wanted to scream and tell everyone I had a sister living in Michigan where the green trees are everywhere.

"Is this heaven?" I asked my mom, then I added, "How come these trees and that grass don't grow here?"

She didn't answer.

As I went through all the pictures, more memories came back, memories blocked by my anger, war trauma, and the malnutrition that I'd endured in the years since her departure.

She used to feed me my favorite meal: Makloba (red

rice with beef, potatoes, and eggplants.) She used to pretend her hand was a train, and I had to eat what was on the spoon before the train passed and missed my mouth. I never failed to hop on the train.

The day she left, we were on the second-floor roof, where we used to have our summer mattresses, and she cried while massaging my dark hair. I never asked her what was wrong. I hugged her, expressing my sympathy without any words, and a few minutes later, my mom called her away.

Lena hugged me and said, "I love you, Habibi." And she was gone.

My anger after Lena's sudden departure from my life was partially to blame for my blocked memories of her. I didn't understand what I'd done wrong or why Lena had left me and had never come back. But now it was clear to me, and I didn't blame her.

Jon: I want you to smile. This was not the worst thing that ever happened to me.

CHAPTER

Ten

The First Day of School

Baghdad, 1991
Adam: seven years old

The usual morning prayers blared through the giant speakers at the top of the mosque's tower, waking me at 4 a.m.

"Allah Akbar. Allah Akbar." *God is great.*

My windows were still taped in case of an unexpected airstrike, but neither the window nor the tape prevented the male voice from penetrating my room. I threw a pillow at my window.

I wish the airstrike had hit him instead of the kids that were burned alive.

I cringed, immediately not proud of my evil thought.

The mosque was only a few blocks away from our

house, and the repetitive prayers invaded my ears without permission frequently throughout the day.

My first day of school was in less than three hours, and I couldn't go back to sleep, so I got up and went to my parents' room.

"What's wrong, Adam?" my mom's voice called as I peeked around the door into their room.

I replied, "I can't sleep. The scary voice ... it's too loud today."

She stepped out of her room and walked me back to my bed. "Try to close your eyes and ignore the noise. You'll be fine. I do it all the time."

As I lay down on my bed with my eyes closed, my anxiety about my first day of school increased. Today would be the first day I would speak Arabic without Rana or Dad around to rescue me if I failed to communicate effectively.

I must have fallen asleep eventually, because I woke again at six, and then I started getting ready for school. My mom gave me a beaten, old, yellow handbag that used to be Rami's—all the characters and words had mostly faded away, but I was sure that, originally, the figures were famous cartoon characters from the Al-Shabab channel.

As I held open the bag for her, my mom stuffed it with books, before she went to start making breakfast. We no longer needed the Ala-eldean heater to cook our breakfast, and I didn't miss those days. We had the stove running again, and we had enough gas tanks to cover us for at least a few weeks.

All of my siblings were awake now, and all six of us were getting ready for school. Rami, Reem, and I would be going to the same elementary school this year, but once Reem hit the age of twelve, they would separate her from the boys until she went to college. After all, it was a Muslim country. We were lucky girls were allowed to go to school with us when we were kids or when we went to college—in other Muslim countries, those options were forbidden too.

"This is your hummus sandwich," Mom said. "I'll place it in the second pouch of your bag. Eat it on your second break, which is your lunch break, and don't let anyone else eat it, okay?"

She waited for my response. I nodded.

I walked toward the main door of our house, a sudden quickness to my steps as I grew more excited. I started wondering who I would meet and how it would go, but when I thought of speaking Arabic, my steps faltered a bit.

My mom caught me before I was out the door and said, "Hold on grasshopper. Close the zipper tight or your sandwich will fall out." She turned toward Reem and added, "Take care of Adam and check on him every break. Also, make sure you guys leave together. No one is allowed to walk by himself, understood?"

Reem did not sound excited by her new assignment, but she said, "Okay," and kept walking.

After a few minutes of walking, I asked, "How far do we have to walk?"

Reem didn't comment, but Rami didn't hesitate to answer immediately. "It's ten minutes to the bus stop. The bus will take another fifteen minutes."

Since I was a fast walker, Reem and Rami fell behind me.

Reem disapproved of my behavior. "Hey, wait up! What did mom say earlier? No one is allowed to walk by himself."

Of course, I responded by walking faster.
Rami grinned and caught up with my brisk pace. Eventually, Reem caught up with us too, unhappy with how we'd acted.

Rami and I laughed, satisfied with Reem's sour expression.

But once we got on the bus, Rami's expression changed. "Oh God, I don't want to go to school."

His statement surprised me. He'd never mentioned anything about not liking school.

"Why don't you want to go?" I asked.

Rami pouted as he explained, "Because I hate school. All the people there are rude."

"Why did you never mention this at home?"

"Of course, I wouldn't mention it at home. I don't want to be lectured by Mom!"

The bus dropped us a few blocks away from the school, and we started walking again. As we approached the school's front door, hundreds of other students did the same. No one rushed. They all walked slow, and everyone had a grumpy face.

"This is not a good sign," I told Rami, but he ignored me.

As we walked closer to the front door, I noticed a big sign above it with five Arabic words I couldn't read.

I asked my brother, "Rami, what does that sign say?"

He replied with a mocking tone, "It's the school's name."

Reem interjected, "It says, 'School of Khalid Bin Alwaleed.'"

Rami rolled his eyes. "Oh God, he will never make it here."

I ignored him, and looked to Reem, so she could explain the meaning of the name, but we'd run out of time—we were already inside the school.

Rami went toward his classroom and shouted, "See you at 1 p.m. by the door. Don't be late. Otherwise, I'll leave both of you!"

"No, you won't, or I'll tell Mom," Reem responded, but neither of us were sure if Rami would listen to her.

Reem held my hand and said, "Let's go. We'll need to be at the square field to line up, and from there, they'll take us to our classes."

I asked, "Why the field?"

"To pay our respects to the flag and Saddam Hussein, and to sing the anthem before school starts. This will be our routine every day. C'mon, they'll punish us if we're late!"

We continued walking, and kids started lining up in rows, side-by-side, in the square field, each grade separated by a sign.

My sister took me to one of the rows, and she said, "This is the first-grade section, every morning you'll stand here and pair with someone, okay?" She waited for me to nod, and then she pointed her finger at a section nearly a quarter mile away and said quickly, "I will be over there in the sixth-grade row."

I nodded.

"Okay," she said, sighing. "Good luck, Adam." And she left.

I examined the area around me. The other first-grade kids seemed as confused as me. But the second graders, in the section next to us, seemed less chaotic—they already knew what they were doing. The school bell rang, and a few minutes later, around twenty teachers started gathering in front of the kids, a flagpole between them and us.

A man approached the pole and started raising the Iraqi flag.

A woman behind him, who seemed angry for no reason, yelled, "All in one voice!" And she started singing the Iraq anthem.

All the kids were singing along with her loudly except the first graders. I moved my mouth, faking my participation. I didn't want test what would happen if I didn't participate. All the kids around me were doing the same.

After the anthem, the man who'd raised the flag

start yelling the words I would listen to for the next twelve years.

"Our goals?" he shouted.

"One united Arabic nation," the kids responded.

The man shouted again, "Our values?"

"Unity, freedom, socialism," the kids said even louder.

"Our party?"

"The Arab Socialist Ba'ath Party."

"Our leader?"

"Saddam Hussein."

They recitation ended with all the kids shouting and clapping their hands.

What the *hell* had I just witnessed? The kids had all behaved robotically, with no life at all, while shouting those words. How was that possible?

The kid that I paired with spoke in Arabic, and I only understood some of it as he said, "In few days, we'll all have to say those words or they'll punish us and hit our palms with a wooden paddle. My brother told me."

I didn't want to listen to him say anything else, so I stopped paying attention. My classmates were all talking to each other, and we stood out from the other lifeless, robotic groups in the square field.

The man who'd shouted the questions at us pointed at our section and said, "You all, do not move! Stay here!" His eyebrows were crossed downward, and his eyes were open wide.

All of us first graders froze in our section and waited. Reem's section had already marched toward the building where the classrooms were located. Suddenly, I wanted to be with her, and I started shaking. My bag felt heavier, and my desire to explore more of the school had withered away. We waited until our section was the only one remaining in the square field.

The man walked closer to us and started speaking, "Are you all aware of who I am?"

A boy behind me coughed and said under his breath, "We don't care." Everyone heard the boy, and suddenly, all the other students in my group went quiet.

The man's face grew angry as he took a few steps toward me. "You, come down here!"

I understood what he'd said, but I ignored the request. As he walked toward my row, my heartbeat started rising. In those few seconds, I told myself I needed to calm down because he wasn't rushing toward me, but when he reached me, he gripped my tiny arm—hard. My water bottle and my bag slammed to the ground.

He's going to rip my arm from my body, I told myself, as the man dragged me to the front of the first-grade line. I glanced at the kid behind me, who smirked without any sign of fear or regret.

I tried to tell the man it wasn't me, but I forgot how to say the words in Arabic, so I spoke in Aramaic.

"Le wen ana," I said. *It wasn't me.*

No one understood what I'd said, and the other kids erupted into broken laughter.

The man turned furious. He was not aware I couldn't speak his language, and he struck my face with his gigantic hands. I fell to the ground.

The man yelled at me, "Get up! You think you are funny?"

The strength of his slap caused me to forget what was happening for a few seconds. He gripped the front of my shirt and made me stand again. He yanked my right hand forward and smacked it hard with the wooden paddle—twice. He did the same to my other hand. I fell to the ground again, powerless, and in great pain.

"I am the principal's assistant," he roared. "If your parents did not teach you how to behave at your home, this is a perfect place for you. I will make sure you understand what respect means."

He turned and faced the first-grade group. "If any one of you talks or makes a single sound during the anthem, I will make sure every single one of you gets what this boy received." He pointed at me on the ground. "Do you understand?"

I tried to catch my breath and stand up, but dizziness from the beating sent me back into the dirt.

A woman approached me and said, "Come here, son. You shouldn't make fun of your elders, and hopefully, next time, you won't, so you will avoid any more punishments."

I didn't respond. What was the point? She wouldn't understand me.

She dusted off my clothes and told me to sit on one of the bricks to rest. She picked up my bag and water bottle and brought them to me. "Drink this."

"Thank you," I said in Arabic. My words faltered— trembled with pain and humiliation.

"What is your name?" she asked.

My eyes stayed on the ground, ashamed of how

we'd met. "Adam," I said quietly.

She smiled. "I'm Ms. Meriam, and I am an English teacher."

"What is English?" I said more to myself than her, but she heard me, and I immediately regretted the words. Would she punish me for asking a stupid question?

She laughed. "It's another language all kids must start learning when they reach the age of eleven."

I didn't respond. I didn't want to learn another language.

Ms. Meriam said, "Let's go. I'll walk you to your class."

I glanced around, and there were no kids. I'd lost track of time and wasn't sure how long we'd been standing there.

"Do you want to rest? I can take you to my office to relax a bit more."

"Can I go home?" I asked her.

"What?" Ms. Meriam didn't understand. I'd said "home" in Aramaic instead of Arabic.

"Can I go home?" This time I fixed the last word of my question.

"Oh, honey, no, you can't, but I promise, it's not

that bad. As long you listen and behave respectfully, you'll stay out of the trouble." She held my hand
and wiped my tears. "No matter what happens to us
sometimes, we must always forgive and do our best."
Her smile never left her face.

How does she exist in this zombie land of a school?
I asked myself.

She said again, excitedly this time, "Come on, let's
go!"

We started walking toward the class. Ms. Meriam
carried my handbag and my bottle of water. I stared at
the ground the whole time, wishing it would just open
and swallow me.

"We are here," Ms. Meriam said. She knocked
on the mahogany-wood door, but no one answered.
She finally opened the door, and the students were in
there by themselves with no teacher. "Stand up!" Ms.
Meriam demanded, suddenly sounding like a different
person.

All the students stood up, reciting words in one
voice, "Long live our great leader, Saddam Hussein!"

"Sit down!" Ms. Meriam responded.

All the students said again as they sat, "Long live
our Baath party!"

Whatever the words meant, I didn't like the behavior—it reminded me of the loud morning prayers, but now I might have to be the one who performed the recitations.

Ms. Meriam asked a student, "Ahmad, where is Mr. Ali?"

"He went to the first-grade class, section B," Ahmad said. "He is double-booked today. He told us to read five pages of the history book while he is covering the other class."

Ms. Meriam thanked him, and we continued down the hall to another classroom. She opened the door and told the students to stand up. No one moved. They stared at her, not knowing what they should do. They were the students who'd been with me earlier.

"Oh God, these kids will need a tremendous amount of training," Ms. Meriam mumbled. "Okay, silent, everyone." She asked the kid who sat by himself on the first seat, "Where is your teacher?"

He was the same kid who'd made the comment on the square field, and he responded to Ms. Meriam, "How should I know?"

A cheerful girl behind him responded without hesitation, "Ms. he took the kid who sat next to

Hareth"—she pointed at the wild, trouble kid—"to the principal's office. He was crying hysterically, so Mr. Ali had to go with him. He'll be back."

Ms. Meriam thanked the girl and asked Hareth, "So, why did you not know? The kid sat right next to you, correct?"

He stared at Ms. Meriam, his face was angled toward the ground, but his eyes still looked up at her.

Her eyebrows were crossed in anger. "If you try to lie again, you will be punished."

Ms. Meriam rested her hand on my tiny shoulder. "Okay, dear, I will leave you here. You can sit in the first seat here until Mr. Ali returns." She placed my belongings next to Hareth. "Good luck, love," she said as she smiled and walked away.

As soon the door closed, Hareth turned into a wild kid again and threw my bag and water bottle to the ground. He told me, "You will not set your stuff next to me, or I'll send you home crying too!"

I responded with curse words I'd inherited from Amar at home.

"What did you say?" Hareth looked at me funny. "You are weird. What language is that?"

I wanted to tell him it was a blessed

language—God's language—but I stopped.

The cheerful girl behind us commented, "My dad told me that is a sinner's language!"

I gazed at her, and I managed to tell her in Arabic, "Your face is a sin."

The class laughed at her.

Hareth continued, "You're not welcome here. We speak Arabic, not a sinner's language!"

I snapped back, "I don't care what you speak. I can talk how I want!"

Everyone in the class started staring at me as if they hated me and my accent. I looked around at everyone, they were all making fun of me and mimicking my words. But I didn't stop speaking until Hareth gripped my collar in one hand and launched his other hand toward my face.

A familiar voice in the background yelled, "Hareth, sit back down!" Then the voice said, "Adam?"

I turned, and it was Mr. Ali from my father's barbershop standing by the wood door. It surprised me at first, but it was also a relief to see a familiar face.

He walked toward me and rested his big palm on my tiny shoulder. "I wasn't aware you'd be coming to school this year. I thought you were younger."

I didn't respond to him, but I smiled awkwardly.

He turned toward Hareth and said, "What is wrong? Why were you trying to hit him?"

Hareth responded, "Mr. Ali, he was speaking a weird language, and he demanded we speak it too.

According to Saher's dad, his language is a sinner's language."

The cheerful girl, Saher, nodded her head in agreement.

"If you ever try to hit another kid again, for whatever reason, I will turn your hand into nothing but bloody red skin," Mr. Ali threatened him.

I could tell how much the class hated the fact Mr. Ali was protecting me.

One student whispered to another, "How do all the teachers know him?"

"Adam, come and sit by me," Mr. Ali said, and I agreed.

We sat at his desk, and he said to me, "It may be difficult at first, Adam, but I want you to try to speak Arabic at school. Otherwise, the kids will be annoyed with you, and you will have trouble. Understand?"

I nodded, but I didn't understand why a language

that was considered blessed in my home, was considered a sinner's language at school.

Jon: I want you to smile. My first day of school was not the worst thing that ever happened to me.

CHAPTER
Eleven

Hate and Religion

Baghdad, 1994
Adam: ten years old

By the age of ten, I was able to speak Arabic perfectly. My blessed, Aramaic accent had faded away. In fact, my teachers considered me one of the best students in the subject of Arabic grammar, and I'd started writing my own poems in Arabic.

So, my suffering wasn't because of my language anymore, but the struggle I had with people accepting my religion was real and ever-present. My middle name Putrus, exposed me as a Christian. Only Christians named their kids Putrus, which was a version of the original Greek name, Petros, meaning "stone" or "rock." In English, Peter was a version of the name

Petros as well. Everyone around me was Muslim, and not all were open-minded, including some teachers. Some students refused to eat with me because they considered me a sinner.

My friend Saad shocked me when he refused part of the apple I'd offered him one day during lunch.

I was aware that some closed-minded Muslims refused to eat with Christians, but I was positive at the time that Saad was not one of those people.

"What is wrong? This is your favorite fruit, isn't it?" I asked.

At first, he hesitated to answer, but he eventually replied with honesty, "Sorry, Adam, my faith does not allow me to accept food from Christians because you are considered a "Moshrek," a sinner in our religion, and it is forbidden for us to eat what you offer."

How had I not noticed? The open-minded Muslim who always played soccer with me, who gossiped about teachers and other students with me, thought of me as a sinner.

My devastation controlled me in that moment, and I could not respond to him with anything but anger. "I thought you weren't like others, but you are exactly like everyone else, a closed-minded asshole. You are out of my life starting today!" I walked away, and I kept my promise—I never spoke to Saad since.

In that same year, I met my first Christian friend: Anmar. He walked awkwardly, his eyes always facing the ground. However, the shiny cross on his chest claimed my attention, and I approached him immediately. The cross around his neck meant home and family to me.

"Hey, how are you?" I asked him.

He lifted his head up and hesitated to answer.

"Hello," he finally said.

"My name is Adam Putrus." I intentionally said my middle name. I wanted to make sure he was aware I was a Christian too.

His face brightened. "I'm Anmar."

I asked, "Where are you from? I don't remember seeing you here before. Will you be in my class?"

"Yes, I'm not from here. I'm from Mosel. My parents moved here for work." He was shy, and I knew it would cause him trouble with the other kids at school, because they preyed on the weak ones.

"Do you mind if I sit next to you?" I asked, not waiting for him to answer.

"Sure." He hugged himself, and I could tell he was scared.

I continued the conversation, smiling. "I can show you around. I've been at this school for five years. I'm familiar with every corner of it."

"That would be nice."

We instantly become friends. My excitement in meeting him drove me to tell my family about the Christian kid I'd met at school. I finally found someone who would not mind sharing food with me at lunch and would not consider me a sinner, the way most students did.

After a few months, Anmar became the friend I talked to about everything. We agreed on everything, and we didn't mind helping each other. One day we conspired together and came up with a way we could afford to buy a Pepsi, actually it was Anmar's bright idea.

"Adam?" He called my name with a questioning tone.

"What?" I responded while flipping through my boring geography book.

"When was the last time you drank a Pepsi?"

I responded, "I can't remember. I don't want to think about it. As you are well aware, I can't afford it.

Why are you even asking?"

"What if we used our bus money to buy a Pepsi?"

"What do you mean? How would we go to school?"

"All we would need to do is to trick our parents and walk three days back and forth instead of using the bus, so on the third day, on our walk home, we could buy a Pepsi." He was smiling, waiting for my response.

"Okay ..." I waited a few seconds to process Anmar's mad suggestion, and I replied, "But my mom always warned me never to walk to school and to always use the bus. It's not safe, plus it would be a total of six miles each day if we walked back and forth. We'd have to leave early. What would we tell our parents?"

"We can say we need to go to school early to study before classes starts," Anmar said.

At first, I told him how crazy his idea was, but as soon as I pictured the cold Pepsi bottle in my hands, and the cool, sweet liquid on my tongue, I weakened and accepted the plan.

"Let's do it," I replied with enthusiasm.

Anmar continued explaining his plan, "Okay, I will meet you by Abu-Hayder's store at 7 a.m. to start our walk. By 8 o'clock, we should arrive at school, but the challenge will be doing this for three days, back and forth, since each Pepsi bottle costs 250 dinars, and our daily bus fare is 100 dinars."

Three whole days. Could I do it?

But I responded, "It's fine. We'll walk for three days. It won't kill us."

Anmar agreed.

We'd walked to and from school for two days, and we'd saved 200 dinars each, but on the third day, exhaustion weighed heavily on Anmar's body and fear was in his eyes.

"What is wrong?" I asked, though I felt his pain because it was also my own.

"I guess my skinny feet are giving out on me—last night they were hurting bad, but today they feel worse. And to be honest, your mom might be right: walking to school is perilous. Have you noticed that creepy old man following us?"

I didn't accept Anmar's defeated tone, so I told him, "My feet hurt too, but we can't give up now. Our prize will be available by the end of the day." I pointed at Abu-Hayder's store as we walked away from our morning meeting place. "We will finally drink those ice-cold Pepsis. Can't you just taste it?"

We shouldn't have been doing what we were doing—not because of the danger presented by people on the streets, though that was scary, but because both of us were too skinny from malnutrition to do six miles of extra walking for three days straight in the heat. Our bodies couldn't afford to expend the extra calories, fragile as they already were, and we struggled to take every step.

"Do you think we should postpone our walk for today?" Anmar asked me. "Give ourselves a chance to rest."

"But we've already come so far, and we would have to wait another day to drink our Pepsis. Let's just keep going," I argued, hoping he would agree.

"Yes, you're right let's just suck it up and continue our mission."

Throughout the day at school, Anmar and I were too tired to focus on our studies. My eyes drifted in and out of focus, and my vision would go momentarily dark every time I stood up from my chair.

On our way home, toward Abu-Hayder's store and our Pepsis, our weak bodies trembled under the heat of the sun, and I saw Anmar rebalance himself several time as his legs nearly give way underneath him.

He wiped sweat from his brow. "God, this is too far."

"Shut up," I said. "You're not helping, Anmar. We're almost there." My lips were dry and cracked from the heat, and I could barely keep my head up. I had to focus on taking one step at a time.

When we finally made it to Abu-Hayder's store, we rushed inside, our excitement overpowering our weariness for a moment.

Anmar pulled out his money out, and so did I. We gave Abu-Hayder our money, and he gave us 50 dinars each in change.

"I can use the change for my next purchase," I told Anmar.

"You need to drink it here at the store. I need the bottles back," Abu-Hayder commented. His face was red with heat, and sweat was gathered above his brows, but he never broke a smile as he handed us the cold Pepsis.

I couldn't stop smiling as the liquid slid down my throat. It was everything I'd imagined and one of the happiest days of my life.

But thinking about it now, Jon, all I feel is sadness. No kid in this world should have to walk for three days, bringing his body to the point of collapse, just to purchase a soda.

Anmar and I continued to be friends until the end of the year.

During finals, while we were waiting for our teacher to give us our results, Anmar had his first brush with religious abuse at the school.

While Hareth stood there waiting with the rest of the class, his eyes hunted for weak prey to feed his boredom, and the cross hanging around Anmar's neck claimed his attention. Without hesitation, he pulled Anmar's golden cross toward his face and spit on it, laughing an evil laugh. Anmar didn't make a sound. He did nothing.

I told Anmar, "Why aren't you defending yourself?"

But Anmar didn't respond. Didn't show any emotion at all.

I lost control of my anger and struck Hareth on his head with my math book, knocking his whole body to the ground. My response shocked him, even though by this time, he was aware of how crazy I could be.

Hareth lifted a hand to his nose and felt the blood there. Then he directed angry, evil eyes at me. He stood up, pinching his nose. "I will end your life. You will pay for this with blood, Christian shit!" And then he rushed out of the class holding his noise.

I asked Anmar, "What the hell is wrong with you? Why did you let him spit on your cross?"

Anmar ignored me.

"Are you seriously not going to say anything?" At this point, my anger at Hareth, at the injustices that had followed me my entire life, turned on Anmar. I spat at him, "How about thank you, Adam?"

"You shouldn't have hit him, Adam. That isn't what Christians do. Plus, what did you think you accomplished by hitting him? Look around. We are surrounded by Muslims on every side. They make up ninety-nine percent of the population here in this country and at this school." He shook his head. "And they will always take his side, not yours."

"Well, sorry, Anmar, but Christians are not cowards. I'd rather be killed than live a life where people spit on my cross. Also, if you aren't willing to defend your cross, what don't you just hide it under your shirt? Haven't you ever wondered why I keep mine tucked away?"

Anmar just walked away, leaving me shocked and speechless.

I'd responded to bullying with a bullying act, but I'd

known Hareth for years, and if I didn't stop him, he'd continue to abuse Anmar. I couldn't believe Anmar couldn't recognize that truth.

This time, though, I'd humiliated Hareth in front of everyone, and he wanted nothing but revenge. As soon I received my passing test result, I headed home to avoid Hareth, hoping that his anger would fade away by tomorrow.

My total passing score was a 90 percent, and I couldn't wait to show mom and dad my achievement. I walked outside, holding my graded paper proudly, taking a shortcut across the sand field by the classrooms.

An angry voice called out from behind me. I turned, and I noticed an older, heavyweight kid coming closer.

"Are you Adam?" he said.

"Yes?" I answered, trying to place him.

Two other kids appeared behind the first kid—Hareth and someone else.

I knew what this was: revenge. I wasn't sure if I could take them all, but I would die trying. I started preparing my strength, fueling myself with the hate and anger I'd accumulated over the past four years of abuse at this school. But that was my biggest mistake—gaining strength from hatred would only wear me out before my enemy.

The big guy ran toward me, and with his massive hand, he struck my face and knocked me to the ground. A buzz invaded my ears, and the pleasant earthy smell of the sand in my face didn't stop the pain swelling in my head. Blood poured from my nose and mouth onto the sand, turning the sand an ugly, dark-brown color. The other kids kicked my stomach as I lay there, and though I wanted to stand up, to fight back with everything I had, I didn't have the chance.

Hareth's hand reached for the thick, silver cross that dangled from a chain under my shirt, and then used it to drag me through the abrasive sand on my stomach. Like a dog being pulled by his color, Hareth pulled me forward so the chain dug into the skin on the back of my neck. I had no power to stop him. While he pulled, the other two kids continued kicking.

I glanced at Anmar as he walked toward the door of the main exit, and he caught my eye, but left as if he hadn't seen me at all, as if I didn't exist.

I squeezed my eyes closed, not knowing what hurt more the beating I was enduring or the cowardice of

my friend Anmar? A tear slipped down my cheek—
both hurt equally.

There were no teachers around to stop my abusers,
and I lay there hoping the thick, silver chain would
break so I could breathe.

"Okay, guys, he's had enough," the big kid said.

But they continued for another few minutes, and
the big kid yelled louder this time, "He's choking! His
blood is everywhere!"

Blood poured from my nose, and mouth, dribbled
from the abrasions on my neck and stomach, when
finally, the thick chain broke. Hareth held it, spit on
it, then threw it on my head and walked away.

I lay hopeless in the sand, blood all over my white
shirt, my graded paper in pieces. There was nothing to
show my mom and dad, except blood and the failure
of their holy cross to protect me. Because the cross
hadn't protected me, as my mom had assured me it
would.

My brows furrowed, disappointment swimming
in my thoughts. I finally stood up and picked the
cross out of the sand. My neck ached as I moved and
was tender to the touch when I ran my fingers along
the back, feeling for something I already knew was

there—marks from my cross's chain gouged deep into my skin.

I was in no shape to walk, but I'd missed the bus, so there was no other option. I gathered all the strength I had left, but I ended up fainting a few blocks away from our house.

Later, Rami told me that our neighbor's kids had found me and called my mom. But I only remembered waking up the next day with a white bandage around my neck and a clean shirt on, no trace of the blood I'd been covered in the day before.

"Mom Adam is awake," Rami announced.

Both my parents were there, and they had plenty of questions.

"How do you feel, honey?" my mom asked.

"Do you want to drink some water?" my father questioned.

"Yes, water please," I said, and I downed the whole glass they gave to me.

"It's probably too early to ask, but do you remember who attacked you?" my mom edged.

As usual, my father followed her question with more questions. "Did anyone witness this? Were you at school or on the street when this happened?"

"I need to rest," I said. "Please, give me space." I didn't plan on ever giving them the answers they wanted.

I was questioning my own actions. I should never have defended Anmar or Christianity. I should have accepted the fact that I was a member of a minority religion, and my faith and I would never be welcome in this country, city, or school. But how could I explain that to my parents?

I continued refusing to tell them what had happened or who had done this to me. I didn't want to drag them into my issues, and I hoped they would, eventually, let me solve it on my own.

My dad, Mom, Rami, Amar, Nabeel, and Reem all tried to extract the information from me, but they all failed. My stubborn silence was stronger than their determination, and my dignity would not let me show them my weakness.

My mom and dad became so worried about my behavior that my dad finally told my mom he was going to go to school tomorrow and investigate what had happened.

He wouldn't find out. There were no witnesses, other than Anmar, but he was too much of a coward to become involved.

I continued hoping my family would let it go, until while lying in bed, Rana approached me. She was the only one who never asked me what'd happened.

"Hi," Rana said.

I didn't reply. I didn't want her to ask the same questions I'd already been asked a hundred times.

"You want to check out what I bought you?" She showed me a card with a warrior on it, a warrior riding a horse with one hoof on the neck of a demon-creature with lizard skin. The warrior's sword was embedded in the demon's chest, even though the demon's flames burned up the warrior's left arm and along the cross on his chest.

I loved the colorful picture. I asked her, "Who is this?"

Rana smiled. "This is St. Korkees. I want you to have it."

"What is his story?" I asked Rana.

She responded with a sad smile, smoothing my hair, "You lived his story yesterday."

"What do you mean?" I asked.

She added, "Examine the picture closely, Adam, the demon tried to burn him and his cross, but this warrior wouldn't give up the fight. Instead, he struck the beast with his sword. It's similar to how we found you yesterday—the links of your chain burst into your skin. But you didn't give up. You kept the cross and walked home." She sighed and continued, "I believe you're a warrior. I don't know the details of what happened to you yesterday, nor do you have to tell me. But I want you to know you are brave in my eyes no matter what happened. I want you to understand that you are not alone in this fight, and whoever is trying to put you down, we must fight and defeat them together."

I looked up at her and asked, "Would I still be a hero in your eyes if I told you I'd started hating the cross, because it brings me nothing but pain and suffering?"

Rana said, "The cross and religion aren't the problem—people are. Some people cannot live in peace. They have nothing to offer but hate. Sadly, it is what they are good at, but it does not mean we should let them change our lives or dictate how we want to live them."

I hung my head low, my voice sounding defeated to my own ears as I whispered, "I'm tired, and I'm afraid I can't be the warrior anymore."

Rana held my shoulders. "That's why we are here. We're your family. We may not be able to change people, but together, we can expose their hate and stop them."

My sister's compelling words had me expelling the whole story. The next day my dad went to school and gave Hareth's name to the principal, and after an investigation, they found out who the other two kids had been. All three of them were suspended from school for a week.

Unfortunately, suspension was only a temporary fix. The real issue was coming from the kids' homes, the upbringing they were receiving from their parents. These kids were only a reflection of how they were raised and what their families had taught them growing up. Anyone who didn't practice Islam was a sinner, in their eyes, and didn't deserve to live.

Jon: I want you to smile. This was not the worst thing that ever happened to me.

CHAPTER
Twelve

No Power. No Life.

Baghdad, 1995
Adam: eleven years old

"It's time to leave this house!" my dad announced early on a Friday morning—June the 2nd, 1995.

All of us siblings were shocked, except for Nabeel and Rana, who'd already known what our dad was planning. But no one else said anything at first, thinking it was a silly joke.

My brother Amar broke the silence. "Are you for real?"

"I am for real," my father responded sadly, with my mom by his side.

Reem followed Amar with another question. "What do you mean? To where? What about school? I'm not changing my friends now!"

Before she could continue with more questions, my father cut her off. "Well, the good news is it is in the area, but it's an apartment. It only has two bedrooms, so some of us will have to sleep in the living room at night."

"We're moving? To a small apartment?" Reem asked again, disbelieving. "For the love of God, this house is bigger than that, and it is *already* crowded. I can't imagine how it will be in an apartment! Who made this decision?"

Rana added some positive news, trying to cheer us up. "It's a lovely apartment on the second floor with a big balcony around all the rooms. We can use the balcony as our sleeping grounds in the summer, and the apartment is right in front of the new popsicle shop, Almahaba!"

Rami smiled, and his eyes widened. "Oh man, I love that place. They have a good peach popsicle. It's the only place that has it."

I had mixed feelings. I re-examined the faces in the room again. My parents' expressions were gloomy. Reem and Amar were annoyed. Rana and Nabeel were doing their best to stay positive and prepare us for the change, and Rami was still distracted by the popsicle comment.

I had many bad memories is this house. Maybe if we moved, I wouldn't have nightmares about bombs falling on our house or watching my family get killed. Maybe if we moved, I'd meet new people, since our current neighbors were mean kids. Maybe if we moved, the loud Muslim prayers through the loudspeakers wouldn't wake me up in the middle of the night. Maybe if we moved, we could afford to buy a popsicle and maybe even a Pepsi too. Maybe was a weak word used to revive broken hopes. It was a desperate word, but it temporarily gave my soul peace.

"I can't wait, Mom!" I said loudly.

Mom's face blossomed with a smile.

Moving to sit next to her, I added, "When we are moving?"

"Next week, hopefully." My mom brushed my short, silky black hair backward and asked, "Are you excited?"

"Yes, Mom!"

I made my mom smile again with my response.

By the end of the week, all our stuff was packed up, and we started moving into our new apartment.

As we approached the building for the first time, my dad said, "This building is only a few years old, isn't that great?"

He examined our faces, but no one was impressed.

For some reason, the building leaned forward, and Reem commented with a sarcastic tone, "Great, we are literally moving to the Pisa building. Is it even safe?"

My dad responded, "It's only few years old. It can't be that bad."

The stairs going up to our apartment were uneven and made of cement with no tiles or other designs on them, only steps. Whoever had built this place, had clearly rushed through the process. Reem's question was legitimate.

"Are you sure it's safe?" I asked.

As we climbed the stairs, my dad said, "Don't worry, guys, it's safe. They just didn't spend much time making it look pretty. The issues are only cosmetic."

I wasn't sure I agreed.

After climbing two floors, we finally arrived at our apartment from the entrance through the balcony.

After a few trips, we'd moved most of our stuff in, and by nighttime we were done. We sat on the floor of the living room, using it as a dining room. We did not own a dining table, so instead, my mom had us sit in a circle on the ground surrounding the Biryani dish. She didn't have enough chicken to feed everyone, but she did the best she could.

For some reason, it didn't strike me as a wrong or odd situation. Not having enough food and not eating what I desired was perfectly normal. It didn't register as a struggle to me. It was just our way of living. I was also fortunate enough that I was able to compare our circumstances to our neighbors'. Most of them lived on white rice, because they couldn't afford any meat at all.

After living in the apartment for few days, we discovered a major problem with running water. It was a common issue for the people who lived above the first level of the apartment building. The water flow was so weak that we had to buy a water pump and place it on the ground level to push water up to our apartment. But the water pump worked only on one condition: when there was electricity. And unfortunately, the power only worked for a few hours at a time.

"Were you aware of this issue?" my mom asked my dad at dinner.

"Yes, but did we have any other options?"

"I can't do everything I need to in a few hours. We need get a big water tank and place it in our balcony."

My dad agreed, and the next day he brought one big tank and few smaller ones. But the tanks couldn't be filled in a few hours by our pump. So, we did what our neighbors were doing. My mom suggested using a few small, handheld buckets of water to get water from the ground level, and she explained that we would need to make trips to fill at least half tank a day. Since it was my school break, I had no option but to be part of her project.

In fact, in the summer, I had two options—either go with my dad to work and clean chopped hair from the floor or stay home and haul water from the ground level to the second floor. I wanted to avoid cleaning stranger's hair, so I helped my mom.

The first day I decided to stay home and make trips to fill up our water tank, my mom handed me a bucket half my size and said worriedly, "Make sure to take a break. It's a big bucket. I don't want you to hurt yourself. Remember, the task is to fill up the tank without hurting yourself or others."

"I'll be fine," I grumbled, ignoring her warnings.

I took the bucket and climbed down the stairs to the ground floor where the main water faucet was located. I found two of my neighbors, nearly my age, waiting in line, and in front of them was an old lady.

"Good morning," I greeted everyone.

Everyone responded politely, greeting me as well.

As we waited, the old lady was hardly able to stand on her feet as she filled her bucket. Her patience eventually collapsed, and she commented, "No wonder the water is not going to our floor. It's barely coming through on the ground floor."

She wiped the sweat from her forehead, and as soon she finished, she tottered toward the stairs with her bucket, but she didn't make it much further. She stopped and sat on the uneven, cement first step to catch her breath.

I walked toward her and asked, "Are you okay, ma'am?"

She smiled. "I'm okay, son. God bless you."

"Do you want me to take your bucket to your apartment?"

"It's heavy, son. I don't want you to hurt yourself. I live on the second floor."

The struggle she was facing at her age, trying to

carry the heavy bucket of water broke my heart. Her weary bones had defeated her, and I could see the helplessness in her eyes. I insisted on carrying the bucket for her, and she agreed.

"What is your name?" she asked.

"Adam," I responded. "Wait for a second, ma'am."

I walked up to the two kids in line by the faucet, and I placed my empty bucket in my spot, asking them to hold my spot until I came back. I rushed back to the old lady, and as soon I held the metal handle of the heavy water bucket in my hands, I realized it was not going to be an easy task, but I pretended it didn't bother me, and I tried to distract her with questions.

"Do you have any kids, ma'am?"

"I'm Am Maher, by the way," she said, using her own name to answer my question.

In Iraq, "Am" means mother, and used as a name, "Am" was typically followed by the name of the mother's oldest son or daughter.

"My husband died in the war with Iran," she went on. "And my one son, Maher, died in the last Gulf War. I moved from Basra to be closer to my sister." Her voice was filled with the pain of what she'd lost, her words broken as she explained the story. "They died years ago." But her pain had never gone away. Her husband and son had been killed by the same man-made evil: *war.*

"Sorry to hear it, may God have mercy on their souls."

"Thank you, Adam, you are such a sweet boy."

I made it a up a few steps, but the bucket was heavy enough that I couldn't move consistently without setting it on the floor to rest. I feared the metal handle would cut through my small, eleven-year-old fingers.

"Are you okay?" she asked me.

"Yes," I lied.

I came up with a technique, setting the bucket down every two steps to rest my hand for a quick second. I continued that rhythm until I arrived at Am Maher's apartment, and we poured the bucket into her quarter-filled tank.

"This is enough for me. Thank you," she said.

"Are you sure? I can haul you a few more buckets if you want."

"The quarter tank is more than enough, son. A lady of my age needs to live for a day at a time. The angels are probably coming here to claim my soul any minute." She started laughing at her own joke.

I added with innocent excitement, "You can consider me your son, Maher. If you need anything, I will be more than happy to help. I live on the right side of the floor. It's the apartment with a white, metal door."

I'd meant to make her happy, but she broke into tears.

She hugged me and said, "You remind me of my son, Maher. He had your dark hair, and he was as kind as you are. I wish the men who controlled the wars had the same innocent hearts as you and Maher, then this would be a better world."

She thanked me again, and I walked back downstairs to complete my initial task. It was my turn to fill out my bucket, and the kid in front of me had saved my spot. Two other kids were waiting behind my bucket, and as soon as I passed them, they both looked at me with expressions that said, "Hey, *what the hell?*"

So, I told them, "Sorry guys, but I had to help Am Maher."

They said nothing.

I made twenty trips up and down, filling the tank, but the tank was not near half full. On my last trip, my feet were shaking, and my hands were too weak to hold the bucket. My two-step technique wasn't effective anymore. It was too late to give up now, so I forced myself to continue, but my skinny legs couldn't handle the effort, and I collapsed. I tried to save the bucket by hugging it as I fell, but it didn't work. I end up pouring the water all over my face and upper body. I returned home soaked in water, dragging my empty bucket.

My mom yelled, "What happened?"

"What you think?" I responded.

"Are you okay? Did you get hurt?" my mom asked.

"No, I'm fine. I need to change."

"Okay, tell Rami it is his turn to fetch water."

We continued preforming this same task all summer. I became close to our elderly neighbor, Am Maher. And my mom never figured out why it took me so much longer to haul the buckets of water than it did Rami.

By the end of the summer, as I poured a bucket into Am Maher's tank, she called my name. "Adam!" She couldn't lift her head straight to talk to me, and she limped over to talk to me.

How could she have ever considered doing the water trips herself?

"Yes," I said. "Are you okay."

Yes, son, but this will be the last bucket you deliver to me today.

I frowned an asked, "Why, did I do something wrong?"

"Not at all, son, one bucket is enough for me. Remember, I'm an old lady, and the angels may be waiting to pick me up already." She smiled and added, "I don't need all this water, no need to give you extra work."

My frown remained, but I tried to smile. "Okay, if that's what you wish."

"I want to give you something," she said, pulling a silver chain with an icon written on it—God.

Am Maher was Muslim, but she was loving and caring towards me in a way only a few had been until that point. Her smile could bring peace to any soul.

Am Maher went on, "I was waiting for Maher to come back from the war to give him this chain, but he never came back." Her lips tightened, and her eyes glistened with tears, but eventually her sadness gave way to a smile. "Maher, I want you to have this!"

I reached out to take the silver chain with the Muslim icon on it, and I didn't hesitate to put it around my neck, even though I was from a Christian family. I wanted her to feel happy. I didn't care if I broke my parents' rules by wearing another religion's symbol.

She pulled my dark hair gently backward and hugged me, saying, "I missed you so much, Maher!" Her happy tears settled on my neck. "*Now, I feel peace. You have the chain, and I want you to wear it. God bless you, son.*"

She made me feel so loved, for a second, I felt like I really was Maher. But I didn't say anything, only smiled and walked away wearing my shiny, silver chain. When I got out of sight, I hid the necklace under my shirt, so my family wouldn't find out—the last thing I needed after all my trips hauling water were more annoying questions from my family.

My regular trips to fill our tank were always brutal, but the pain of that specific day was like no other. The power was off for twelve hours, and our apartment boiled from the excessive heat.

At nighttime, Rana laid the mattresses on the balcony, and I tried to drink water to beat the heat, tried to keep myself hydrated, but it didn't help. I wanted to sleep.

"There's no air, not even a single breeze," I complained aloud to my family, but no one answered me.

I told myself I would die sweating my guts out, and no one could help me. I' lost all patience, because the heat had consumed me. I wanted to jump from the balcony. In the summer, many people jumped from windows or balconies, killing themselves. I'd never understood why, but now I did—they wanted to end their misery and pain.

I started crying, trying to hide my tears.

"What is wrong?" Rana asked.

"What type of question is that?" I barked at her, tears filling my cheeks. "We are literally living in hell, and you're asking me what is wrong?"

"When I was your age, I went through the exact same struggle." Rana wiped my tears. "But I realized that this life is what you want it to be."

"How? I want a breeze right at this moment to come in and kill the heat. I want to breathe. But I can't make it so."

"Close your eyes, Adam," Rana said.

I did what she asked me.

She went on, "The breeze is always there, but focusing on the heat doesn't let you feel it. Every time a breeze passes across your skin, your negativity is keeping you from feeling it. Keep your eyes closed. I want you to stay still. Breathe slowly and wait for the breeze. It will hit every ten to fifteen minutes."

I did what she asked me, and after a few minutes, a tiny breeze hit my forehead gently.

"I felt one, did you?" she asked me.

"Yes, I did," I responded calmly.

"You will face so many things in life, Adam. Your focus must always be on the positive. Remember, there is always something good in every bad story. The good part of our bad story today is the breeze. It visits us every few minutes. We need to be patient to wait for it, feel it, and enjoy it."

I kept my eyes closed, waiting for the second breeze, third breeze, and forth until my body gave up the struggle and fell asleep. Rana's method had worked.

"Adam," my mom called me the next morning. "Please start your water trips. We're out of water already."

"Okay, mom," I said as I picked up my bucket to perform the task.

The first person who crossed my mind was Am Maher. I'd need to provide her more water today, and

I wasn't sure if one bucket had covered her through
the night. I went to check on her before I started my
trips, but there were people gathered outside her
apartment, inside it too.

"What happened?" I asked a man standing by the
door.

The downcast man said, "Am Maher died. Are you
related to her?"

I said, "Yes, I mean no, I'm not a relative, but she is
my friend."

I didn't want to process what he'd said, so I asked,
"She is gone?"

I hoped his answer would change, but it didn't.

"Yes, she is gone"

I reached out to touch the chain she'd given me.

The last thing she'd ever said to me was, "Now,
I feel peace. You have the chain, and I want you to
wear it. God bless you, son."

Happy tears flooded my eyes, and I was pleased
that I'd become part of her peace. Tears of sadness
followed. I would miss Am Maher a lot. I couldn't
change her past, but at least I'd helped ease the pain
of her present.

I whispered to my lost friend, "Your kind smile and

eyes will always be in my heart. You were right—the angels were waiting for you, and you did not need the final bucket. Rest in peace."

Jon: I want you to smile. This was not the worst thing that ever happened to me.

CHAPTER
Thirteen

The Second Separation

Baghdad, early 1998
Adam: fourteen years old

Years of sanctions implemented by the United Nations
and the United States had affected every small detail
of our lives, even our personalities had started changing, especially Amar's. He'd developed a habit of
treating anyone he didn't love with violence. The
anger inside him was no longer hidden, and he'd started to be involved in daily fights.

His bad behavior was at its peak when he came
home with a bloody hand, and our mom and dad
freaked out.

"What have you done this time?" Mom asked him.

Amar, with a nasty attitude, replied, "Nothing, I

had to teach some shit head a lesson."

My dad yelled at him, "Are you out of your mind? Are you aware of what these people could do to us, especially to Christian people like ourselves?"

"Let them try. I will end their lives on the spot," Amar responded with no fear. I believed he was telling the truth—he wouldn't hesitate to end a life if someone crossed him.

My mom started crying. "We didn't raise you to think like that. We didn't raise you to harm people or be a killer."

"Open your eyes and look around you, Mom! We live in a shit-hole with people who have zero respect for us or our family. Why should I respect them?"

"What do you want, Amar?" my dad asked calmly.

"I want you to fix your shit," Anmar yelled, kicking a chair to the ground. "This is all your fault. You kept us here. We should have left this country when we had the chance. All these years, and all you do is to live day-by-day. Have you ever thought about what kind of future we have here? Have you ever wondered what we go through every day? I want to leave this place and never come back!"

My father sounded hopeless. "Are you sure you want

to leave? None of us can join you. Are you sure?"

"Yes, I'm sure. I'm sick of you and this place."

My father said sadly, "I will arrange the papers for you to migrate to Jordan. You'll have to find your way out from there."

"At least you will have done something useful in your life," Anmar responded bitterly, and he walked out.

Eighteen years old, and Amar was ready to leave the cage.

My mom turned to my dad. "What are you talking about? You won't really let him go to Jordan, will you? And then what?"

"Trust me," my dad said. "It's best for everyone. Did you see the blood on his hand? He is up to no good, and next time someone could get killed. His anger will dissipate once he leaves and starts his own life. We can't cage and overprotect our kids forever. We need to let him go."

My mom didn't respond, tears sliding down her cheeks.

How would life be without Amar in our house? I asked myself.

We all understood what Amar was going

through—we'd experienced the same stress. But each one of us dealt with it differently. Nabeel dealt with stress by reading as many books as he could. Rana relieved stress by going to church more often and by teaching Bible study. Reem dyed her hair whenever she got the chance, and Rami snuck around to explore dangerous parts of the city, which had given my parents multiple "heart attacks" over the years. But Amar had an aggressive personality, and he couldn't do any of those things. So instead, he'd ended up becoming violent and rebellious.

I dealt with the stress by drawing characters on paper and giving them names and backstories. All the characters had the things I wanted but couldn't afford. They were also loved by everyone regardless of their religion. These characters had houses, electricity, and running water. They ate meat every day, and they drank Pepsi anytime they wanted to, without having to walk miles to save up money. The characters I drew lived in a quiet place without the sounds of bombs or loud mosque prayers. These characters had everything I didn't.

They were my stress relief—my make-believe characters and my fantasies. They distracted me from the real world and everything that was wrong with my life.

A few days passed, and my father walked in with Amar's passport and handed it to him. "Here you go, as I promised."

Amar took the passport, relief on his face but hostility in his voice. "Okay, good, I can arrange my trip. I'm leaving in a week."

My mom said with a nervous tone, "That fast? Let me make arrangements with your uncle in Jordan to see if they have room to host you."

"Fine. But I'm not waiting for more than a week."

Both my parents were terrified to get in his way, so they said nothing. On Wednesday afternoon of the same week, we sat my brother's luggage on the balcony while he sorted through his documents, waiting for the SUV to pick him up.

"Ready?" my dad asked him.

"Yes, I'm ready," Amar said, but he didn't appear to be ready.

My mom sobbed. Nothing killed me inside more than my mom's tears. Her world and my world were being turned upside down, grief tearing us apart inside. Amar's departure affected my siblings too, and they all started crying as we said goodbye. I pretended to be strong and didn't shed any tears, but I wanted to.

Amar was leaving, and I wasn't sure if I'd ever see him again. We'd all heard the stories about refugees dying as they tried to escape through Jordan across the sea into Cyprus and from there into Turkey, and eventually, across the sea into Italy or Greece. Was it possible he'd never make it? Was this the last time we'd ever see him? What would happen to Mom if she found out her son had died? I needed to put a stop to my negative thoughts, to the questions that were attacking my mind.

Amar distracted me when he started walking toward me. He gave me a quick hug and walked away. Tears were on his cheeks. Here he was the toughest man in our family, but vulnerability glistened in his eyes as he prepared to leave his loved ones behind. It was an evil he never should have had to face, but it was also a choice that he knew he had to make.

Jon: I want you to smile. This was not the worst thing that ever happened to me.

CHAPTER
Fourteen

No Fear but Freedom

Baghdad, late 1998
Adam: fourteen years old

Amar made it to Italy. He was brave enough to hop on a small boat and cross the sea. "He's lucky," Nabeel told my mom. "Many people don't make it alive.

My mom made the sign of the cross. "Thank the Lord."

"Do you think it's time for me to follow the same path?" Nabeel asked.

"No, what about your college? And who will help your dad?" My mom would use any excuse in the world to keep us from leaving home.

"College will be over in a month. As soon as I have

my bachelor's degree, I want to leave, Mom. Rami and Adam can help Dad. I can't waste my life anymore." Nabeel sounded like he'd been rehearsing this conversation for a while, and he'd decided that today was a good day to test the waters.

"Talk to your dad when he gets back from work," my mom continued, her tone serious. "But I want to remind you, Amar may have made it to Italy, but not everyone does. And he may never see his family again. I know you are aware of the risks, but I'm going to remind you anyway. We live in a country where the government will show you no mercy if you are caught trying to flee or trying to escape army duty. Keep that in mind."

Nabeel was not backing down from his decision. I could tell he was ready and willing to take the risk, including possible death, as long there was a chance to leave Iraq. I scrutinized Nabeel's expression, the set of his jaw and his determined pose. *Will I ever come to that point? Will I ever share Nabeel's state of mind? Will I be determined to leave no matter the consequences? I mean, we'd been through a lot already. What could be worse?*

As soon my dad arrived home, Nabeel brought

up the subject again. My father stopped him before Nabeel got the chance to say anything else.

"Continue on to get your master's degree," my dad argued. "That way, you'll postpone your army duty for another two years. Plus, you'll have a stronger educational background."

My father knew why Nabeel wanted to leave. Nabeel wanted to leave Iraq, so he could avoid going into the army. I didn't blame him. Army service in Iraq was mandatory, and it was for men only. If you passed high school, you would go on to college, but if you failed high school, at the age of eighteen, the government required you to join the army. The punishment for failing to do so was getting your right ear cut off. You could also be prosecuted for treason, and your family would then be monitored by the government. There were even checkpoints in the streets where men who looked to be of army age were asked for IDs. But if you continued school through college, your army duty was postponed until the age of twenty-two. If you earned a master's degree, it could be delayed even further. But it was mandatory beyond a master's degree.

Young soldiers used to pass by my father's

barbershop walking with their oversized, olive-colored outfits, often with messy hair and pale, sickly-looking skin.

"How can these people possibly protect us?" I asked my dad once. "They don't look like they can even take care of themselves!"

"I don't know, son, but don't you ever ask that question again—not to anyone! We have no right to question the government's decisions! Understood?"

Any questioning of the government's practices, at the time, was considered treason, and often, the penalty for treason was execution. My father wanted to protect us from harm at all costs.

In times of duty, soldiers in Iraq weren't given enough meals throughout the day, and their salaries were unrealistic. A whole month's salary was barely enough to buy three or four meals total, and they usually deployed far from home, so they had no access to friends or family. The leaders said the lack of food taught soldiers how to be tough—as if they hadn't already been struggling their entire lives. To make matters worse, army generals would smuggle soldier's meals and sell them for profit. No one knew if higher-level government officials were aware of the practices or not, but no one dared raise the issue in public, fearing what the punishment would be.

"Sir, I have no money to pay you, but would you please shave my head and beard?" a soldier asked my father one day at the barbershop. The soldier went on, "If I show up at training like this, I will go to jail."

"How far away is your family, son?" my dad asked him.

"They live in Basra," the soldier said. Basra was about 400 miles away from Baghdad.

"You're far from home, son. Come in, I will shave your head and beard."

In Iraq, at the time, it wasn't cheap to own a razor or a trimmer, and not everyone could afford it.

"You know, son, when I was your age. I served in the army too." My father settled into his habit of telling stories as he cut the man's hair, and I listened as if he was telling this story for the first time. My dad continued, "Back in the seventies, my family lived north, but they deployed me all the way down south. To Basra, in fact."

The soldier's face brightened. "How was it back then?"

"Those were good days, son. There were no

sanctions on Iraq, and the country wasn't war-torn yet. Basra was a beautiful city. People were kind and cared about each other there."

"So, you haven't been in any war?" the soldier asked.

"I finished my duties before the war started," my dad explained. "But unfortunately, I lost my brother in the war." His expression had grown sad.

When my dad finished shaving the soldier's head, it was shining. My dad applied after shave cream, and then he started shaving the soldier's beard.

"How many more years do you have left?" my father asked.

"Two more years," the soldier mumbled, afraid to talk because the razer was under his chin.

"Which facility have you been deployed to?"

"Baghdad Aljadeda," the soldier mumbled again, barley was able to move his mouth.

My dad commented, "Oh, yeah, I know where that is." My dad had been living in Baghdad since 1969; he knew where everything was.

After my dad finished, the soldier's cheeks grew pink with embarrassment as he told my dad, "Sir, I can give you 100 dinars. I know it's nothing, but I feel awful not paying for your service."

"No need for any money, son. You're more than welcome anytime. We appreciate your service, and you're greatly valued by us." My father always responded this way—to any soldiers—even if they didn't ask for free services, my father wouldn't take any money from them.

Nabeel, on the other hand, did not love my father's proposal of continuing on to his master's degree, but he didn't have any other good options either. So, he agreed to move on with his degree in engineering and postpone army duty. A few months passed, and the tensions between the Iraqi government and the United States raised again. At the time, Bill Clinton was in the office. Most of us in Iraq preferred the United States Democratic Party, because they tended to mind their own business and avoid wars at all cost. But the prevailing notion did not hold true in this case. They had had enough of Saddam's madness, so they launched airstrikes again for a few days, trying to hit strategic locations where the United States claimed Saddam might be hiding his weapons.

At 9 p.m., on the first day of strikes, Baghdad's city siren roared. It had been a while since I'd heard it, but by then, we were all immune to the sound. We were living in the second-floor apartment, and we had no backyard room to hide in this time. In fact, we didn't even bother going to the lower level. We all stayed in the living room, watching through an untapped, glass window, not caring if it shattered. We were not afraid of dying anymore.

The red lights had once claimed my uncle Mosa's life. I wondered who would die today. As the sound grew louder, hundreds of red lights showered over the city like meteors. Bombs raced across the sky, falling onto the building before me. I had the best view from the window. I still had no fear.

What a beautiful view? I whispered to myself.

Rami heard what I'd said. "You're creeping me out. You know people are dying out there, right? There's nothing beautiful about it!" Rami walked away from the window shaking his head.

His words didn't register with me. I continued staring as the sounds grew louder. Everyone was there: Rana, Reem, Rami, Nabeel and my parents—the only ones missing were Amar and Lena.

We lost power, and the only light was coming from the candles my mom had lit earlier.

"We need to blow out the candles," Reem urged. "We don't want to be seen. They might think we are a target."

They all lay down, careful not to lay beneath the heavy ceiling fan as a small safety measure, but I remained in my position, not fearing any sounds or the bombs.

My family shouted from afar, "What are you doing? Come over here!"

I ignored them. There was no way to escaping the bombs this time. I was certain they'd claim my soul.

I wasn't sure if I'd lost my mind, but it felt right. Nothing mattered anymore. I'd experienced everything except death. We'd been avoiding death since day one of the war. But what if death was the answer to all our suffering?

"It is okay ... It's okay ... I'm ready," I told my family, absently, distantly. But I doubted they'd heard me, not with all the noise.

A voice louder than the bombs yelled from behind me, "What the hell? Snap out of it!" Nabeel was trying to pull me out of the stupor I was in. The scene was scary enough that everyone else was afraid to come by the window to rescue me.

A massive yellow light. It was the mother of all the falling bombs, headed toward a building on the horizon. But another skinny red light launched in quick succession toward the yellow light. They collided—the two missiles—and the sky went as bright as daylight. The burning buildings were easily viewed. The collision that had generated the light, and a cloud of smoke, was followed by a booming sound and intense pressure on our windows. They shattered, throwing me to the ground. Warm blood rushed down my face, blocking my vision.

Sometimes I wished I didn't have a family that I loved so much, so I wouldn't have to worry about losing them to the war or to the ruthless regime. I could only imagine the anger and rage that would evolve in me if any of them were harmed. I understood Amar's rage, in that moment, understood why he'd become a violent person.

"Where's the Candle? I can't see clearly," Rana's voice called out in the darkness. "I don't want to step on shattered glass."

Rami added, "Be careful, Rana. Be careful. Don't step on it!"

"Adam ... Adam ..." Rana raised her voice, trying to

find me, but I couldn't answer her or open my eyes.

Suddenly, it was quiet, peaceful, and I was free of worries. I'd never been so calm in my life. I woke up on a white bed, and there was a small desk sitting off to one side. On top of the desk, was a red book. It was written by me. The title of the book was unclear, and I was not able to read it, because it was written in a foreign language. When I tried to stand up, I didn't use my feet. Instead, my body moved anywhere I wanted to go, using only my eyes.

What freedom! I thought to myself. *Do I have a superpower?*

I stared through the window, and I was able to leave the room by gazing in the direction I wanted to go, easily passing through walls and windows. I was in the sky, staring at the city beneath me. This city was different from the one I'd lived in all my life. Everything was beautiful, clean, and peaceful, with houses like the ones I'd seen in Western movies. Something told me to continue my search to find a specific building, so I examined around, and I found it simply by looking. I was able to transport myself into the building, and all the students I'd met in my childhood were there—and all the teachers and some strangers—standing in rows moving slowly. I greeted the people I was familiar with, without saying any words. I asked them what they were doing just by gazing at them, communicating without using my mouth, but rather, somehow, my eyes. They responded to me likewise.

"Stay in the line, Adam. Wait for your turn." It was Am Maher, and happiness filled my soul as I hugged her.

I did what she asked me to do—I waited. But as I gazed toward the front of the line, I saw a fire. All these people were throwing themselves in the fire to be burned. I yelled, but I had no voice, so I started rushing ahead, waiving at everyone to stop, but no one listened. My childhood friend, Anmar, was there walking toward the fire, ready to through himself in, ignoring my dire warnings. I received no response from him—or anyone else.

I thought to throw myself in first, hoping this would change something or get the rest of them to stop.

I possess a strange power here—I told myself. I can stop the fire. The fire blazed through some people, making them disappear into thin air. But I didn't hesitate to dive toward the fire anyway. The flame tried to reach for me, but instead of consuming me, I turned it into smoke, and it disappeared. Having stopped the fire on one side, and with the people there safe, I turned to the other side. There was more fire, and I dove for it too. I went through all the flames, in the entire building, until I'd turned every single flame into smoke, and everyone was safe.

I wanted to go back to my room to read the book I'd writted. My eyes flew through the sky back to the room.

On the cover of the book was the image of skeleton, and the skeleton yelled at me, "What have you done? What have you done?" The voice got louder and louder, until I opened my eyes again, but this time it was my mom shouting at me. "What have you done?"

I tried to move using my eyes as I'd done earlier, but I couldn't. I came back to my body again. It was heavy and painful. I couldn't move my legs or hands.

"What have you done? Why did you stay by the windows?" my mom shouted again.

I replied, "Sorry, mom, for being selfish, I'm sorry." I don't think she understood what I meant.

I was selfish because I'd wanted to die first. I couldn't watch them die before me.

But my mom hugged my half-paralyzed, bloody body and cried, "Don't be sorry, baby. It's never your fault, It's never your fault."

Jon: I want you to smile. This was not the worst thing that ever happened to me.

CHAPTER
Fifteen

The Army of Illusions

Baghdad, early 1999
Adam: fifteen years old

My mother, siblings, and I were sitting on the balcony, waiting for nature to reward us with a breeze to beat the heat, because the power had been off for the past two hours. Eight years after the hunger vote, our country was still in what we Iraqis called, "the time of the sanctions." Though, at this point, we had a more reliable electricity schedule—power all day except from 2 p.m. to 4 p.m. and from 10 p.m. to midnight. The United States had continued its targeted airstrikes on certain locations within Baghdad. But we'd had a dry spell in the bombing over the past six months, which meant the government was better able to maintain the power stations.

My father came home from work, walking through the rusty, white, metal door with an angry face. He found us all out on the balcony, but his angry gaze was directed at me. "I can't believe, out of all my kids, you would do this to me!"

He was definitely looking at me, but I couldn't fathom what I'd done wrong. The only rebellious thing I'd ever done was when I'd walked to and from school for three days in order to buy a Pepsi, and that had been years ago. I glanced around, looking at everyone else's faces to see if they thought he was talking to me too.

But then my father made himself clear by calling my name, "Adam!"

My mom answered for me, "What are you talking about? What has he done?"

"He'd going to be expelled from school!" my father shouted, his angry eyes still fixed on me. "Why would you do it? Where have you been going for the past seven days? Were you lying to us? Of all my kids, I wouldn't have expected this from you."

My mom defended me, "Impossible, who told you?"

"I received a note from the school saying Adam has missed school for the past seven days, and tomorrow will be his final day before he gets expelled."

My mom said, "There must be some mistake." She turned to look at me, a frown on her face. "Adam? Do you have anything to say for yourself?"

I didn't respond. Instead, I grabbed my ripped, over-used backpack and pulled out my copybook, showing my parents the dated notes I'd taken for the past seven days.

"So, they are mistaken!" my mom said, relieved.

My father gazed at the notes, his brows furrowing. "What the hell is happening at your school? I was angry my whole way home from work for nothing."

"You still need to go with him to school tomorrow and see why they sent the note," my mom told my dad.

Early the next day, my dad and I went to school to investigate further. As we entered the school, my dad's eyes grew wide. "What the hell?" he said.

My dad hadn't visited one of his children's schools in years, and the building looked more like a prison than a school now. All the windows were caged with metal bars, yet glass was still missing from more than a few windows after they'd been shattered during various airstrikes. Before the war, some money was put into the maintenance of school buildings, but virtually no money had been allocated for this purpose since 1990, which meant for the entirety of my educational career, the school buildings where I'd attended classes had been going further and further downhill.

"So, this is how the schools are these days?" my father commented aloud, as he continued walking toward the principal's office.

Teachers were walking around with wooden sticks, yelling at kids for unknown reasons, like they were herding sheep and not students.

"What a zoo!" my father mumbled. He wasn't far off.

We finally arrived at the principal's office, and my father knocked on the half-broken door.

Mr. Jasim, the school's principal, was sitting with his legs crossed reading a newspaper and didn't pay any attention to my father's knock. My father knocked again.

Mr. Jasim finally gave us his attention, peeking his eyes over the newspaper. "Yes! What is it?"

"I'm here to talk about my son, Adam. We received

a notice by mistake, saying you were going expel him from school for not attending classes. He has been attending every day, and he has proof."

Mr. Jasim responded, "Oh, I wrote the letter myself, and I assure you I didn't make a mistake."

How arrogant! I thought.

The principal added, "Today is his last chance!"

"I'm sorry, but what do you mean? I told you he attended all his classes. Why are you saying today is his last day?" My father's tone had changed—he was losing his patience.

"Well, your son did not show up to any of the after-school weapons training classes."

"Weapons training? What is it for?" my dad asked.

"This school is Baath-party owned. All students must be part of it. They are required to learn how to use weapons, and if necessary, go to war."

"War! What are you talking about? He is fifteen!"

"He is old enough to fight and kill to serve the Baath Party." He sat back in his chair and grinned maliciously. "However, no need to panic. You still have the option to leave the school, but as far I'm aware, ninety-nine percent of Baghdad schools are owned by the Baath Party now. There's a school two hours north that doesn't require your son to be trained, but you must take him there and register today, because they don't take students who are expelled from other schools." Mr. Jasim clearly relished being the source of other people's frustration. "So, what will it be, sir? I don't have all day for you and your son."

"I will do it, Mr. Jasim," I said. "I will do the training and learn how to use weapons."

"So, why didn't you show up on the first day if you are willing to join?"

"I wasn't aware it was mandatory, Mr. Jasim." He didn't deserve my respect, but I replied respectfully anyway.

"Oh, it's not mandatory. You have the freedom to refuse at any point, but if you do, you won't have a place at this school." He gathered some papers on his desk and dismissed us. "Okay, make sure you attend at 1:30 p.m. today. That will be all."

I said nothing, but his comment about freedom was similar to the *freedom* I'd heard described in religions—God gave you the freedom to worship Him or not, but if you didn't worship Him then you wouldn't have eternal peace and there wouldn't be a place for you in Heaven. Instead, your soul would be fated for Hell. I'd always wondered where the freedom was in logic like that? There certainly wasn't any freedom for me—I was headed to weapons training.

My father squeezed my shoulder and said, "I'm sorry, Adam, how I can fix this?"

"Don't worry, Dad. I'm not the only one who will be doing this. It's my fault. I should have known what *optional* meant in this country." I smiled and added, "I will be okay, trust me." I wanted to comfort him, but I wasn't very successful.

My father held my shoulder and sadness overcame him. He walked away without saying anything, leaving me at school to begin my day.

At the end of the day, I did what Mr. Jasim had told me to do. I went to the backyard of the school—everyone called it *the mini-desert* or the *back of the school desert*. There were many students there, some standing in line, others dragging heavy weapons through the sand.

A scar-faced guy yelled, "New students stay back to register your names and to sign out your weapons. Don't you dare come over here without a weapon. You don't want me to lose my patience with you animals."

I was instantly afraid of him, so I did what he demanded. I waited in the line of new students to register my name and claim my own weapon.

When it was my turn, the guy sitting at a small desk with a book asked me my name. When I didn't answer immediately, he barked at me again, "Are you deaf, boy? What is your name?"

"I'm sorry, my name is Adam ... Adam Putrus."

"Oh God," he mumbled to himself. "There is no future for this country with these new feminine generations." He examined me from top to bottom with, a disgusted expression on his face, as if I'd done something shameful. "Okay, I need you to sign here to confirm you received the weapon. The weapon must be returned the day after the Army Pride Parade. If you fail to do so, your father will be given a sentence of ten to fifteen years in prison. Also, you will need to take this paper home for your dad to sign, and you must return it to me no later than tomorrow, understood?"

My brain froze for a second. My father's life, literally, depended on this weapon! And yet these words meant nothing to this guy. He'd said the same thing over and over so many times that the words had lost their meaning. I didn't comment or object. I signed the paper, and I took the other one for my dad to sign.

The weapon was Russian-made and called a "Klakinshoof." The length of the weapon matched my height, and it was incredibly heavy. I could barely stand straight holding it. Thankfully, the weapon's strap allowed me to wear it over one shoulder like a backpack, and I was able to lean to the opposite side to balance my weight.

The guy at the desk finally laughed and said, "War will shit you out dead like a speck of dirt."

I ignored his comment, and I walked away toward the group of students who already had their weapons. I stood in the line, giving my shoulder a break by resting my Klakinshoof on the ground. In the front of the line, the guy with scarred face was talking, but I could barely catch what he was saying.

It was already 2 p.m., and the sun was in the middle of the sky, pouring its burning rays down on our heads, trying to turn us into the sand beneath our feet.

I started mimicking the guys in front of me, practicing the moves the instructor had asked us to perform. The instruction was to hold the Klakinshoof on our right sides, shout the words he instructed, and then carry our weapons again on our right shoulders, marching our feet left and right as if we were one soldier. For the next two hours, we were trained how to move our legs and hands in unison, and we were taught how to stand straight. We didn't talk about how to use the weapons at all on the first day of training.

"All right, that is enough for today," the scar-face instructor said. "Tomorrow be ready to learn how to disassemble and reassemble your weapons. You will not leave until you can manage that task within one minute."

As we started dispersing and readying ourselves to leave, the instructor shouted at us again, "Hold! I did not dismiss you yet! You will leave when I say you are dismissed."

I'd already had enough of this guy. *Can't someone use his weapon to shut this guy's mouth?* I thought. But then I remembered that we had no ammunition in our Klakinshoofs, so we couldn't use them even if the thought *had* been more than a passing fancy—which it hadn't.

He made us wait another 5 minutes, then he shouted. "Okay, you are dismissed now."

It was close to 4 p.m., and I was hungry and tired. I had to carry my backpack in addition to the weapon, so even the short walk to the bus station was excruciating.

What a sight we all were, a bunch of high school kids dragging Klakinshoofs along with their backpacks home from school. All for what? So some wealthy people could try to get wealthier? So some maniac could show the world how powerful he was? I wished I could save all the kids around me, but I didn't even have the power to save myself. And, for my family's sake, for the sake of their lives, I shoved aside my rebellious thoughts and didn't think of them again.

The next day I took the document my father had signed and went back to training. This time, the training included more about the weapons themselves.

"Okay, this is how you will need to start disassembling your weapons," the scar-faced instructor announced. Then he showed us how to assemble it again. "As I told you yesterday, this task must be finished in one minute. If you fail, you will do it over and over. I don't care if you stay here for the rest of your life!"

I believed every word he said.

I managed to accomplish the task within my third or fourth try, but not all the students succeeded.

"Are your brains made of a pile of shit?" the scar-faced guy yelled at the kids who were not able to do it. "Do it now! Do it now!" he shouted, getting as close as he could to these kids' faces. "Does that look like how I showed you?"

His voice was getting louder and angrier with each passing second, and the kids who couldn't manage the task were only getting more nervous and becoming clumsier with their weapons.

The instructor humiliated them over and over until everyone was able to achieve the task except one kid in our group. He was skinnier than I was, and though I knew he was older, he looked like he was barely nine. His tiny body couldn't handle the weight of the Klakinshoof, and the heat of the sun had made the metal of the weapon so hot it was burning his fingers. Finally, he collapsed and fainted. He fell flat on the hot sand. No one offered any water or any help, fearing the instructor would punish them.

But I couldn't stay still any longer, I couldn't watch and do nothing. I rushed toward the kid, not caring what Scarface would do to me. For the past eight years, I'd been abused verbally and physically many times over. Another abusive punishment added to my record, from Scarface or whoever, was something I could handle. It didn't matter anymore. All I cared about in that moment was saving this kid from choking on the sand. I pulled his head upward, and I cleaned his face.

"Are you okay? Can you stand up?" I asked the kid as he roused to consciousness.

"I-I'm trying," he said. "Need some water, please." He was mumbling his words, and his pupils were rolling backward—it reminded me of a possessed little girl I'd seen in a scary movie.

I didn't have any water by my side, so I said, "We must return to school and go to the main faucet to drink water. This will help you."

The kid was unresponsive.

The water from the faucet was warm, close to hot, but still better than nothing. I raised my hand above the kid's face to block the burning sun, hoping it would help.

"Can I take him back to school?" I asked the scar-faced guy politely. "He needs water, sir."

The scar-faced instructor didn't show any sympathy. "Who told you that you could leave your position?"

"No one did, Sir," I replied without any regret. I was ready for his abuse.

"In war, you will see your friends die before you, and you must keep the mission as your priority, not your friends. Do you understand?"

I replied with a firm tone as if we were in an actual war, "I understand, Sir."

No mission in the world would force me to ignore any of my friends or family members, nor would it force me to let them face any abuse or death alone. Although, in this case, I'd never met the kid before, nor was he a friend or family member, but it was wrong to leave him on the ground in desperate need of help.

Scarface continued, "Good. I will keep an eye on you. You're lucky your mission today is to save this soldier. Take him back to school and give him water. Tomorrow, if he faints again, don't you dare give him help!" Scarface walked away.

"Okay, you need to stand up. We can finally leave."

He did, and we walked together back to school, me helping him along like he was a real wounded soldier.

He drank the dirty, hot water and washed his face with it as well.

"Sorry, but I'm not allowed to help you tomorrow," I told the kid.

His tone was sad and defeated. "I understand."

"But I can teach you how to disassemble and reassemble the Klakinshoof quickly. It's easy don't let the size of the weapon intimidate you." I was telling him this, but I wasn't sure if he was into it at all.

"Okay, show me how. I don't want to go through this again tomorrow," the kid said.

"Are you sure you want me to show you now?" I asked.

"Yes, please."

I showed him how and he tried it, and this time, with no pressure, he was able to do it within the required time.

"Thank you," he said. "I'm sorry. I didn't get your name."

"My name is Adam."

"I'm Samy."

He shook my hand and we left.

∼

After a few weeks of training, we were finally ready for the Army Pride Parade. "Tomorrow is the Army Pride Parade," the scar-faced instructor announced. "You must all be proud to serve the Baath party. More importantly, you must all be proud to perform for our great leader, Saddam Hussein."

I finally understood why the course had been mandatory. The whole plan was to show off Saddam Hussein's massive army via the media. But the truth was, we weren't his army. Most of the "soldiers" who would be marching in the parade were only kids.

"Don't forget all the lessons we have learned. Be a part of one big, strong body. We must all move the same, and we must all act the same. I also want to add a few other notes for you to remember tomorrow. Don't you dare joke while you are doing the pride march. There will be snipers all over the Army Pride Parade. Their jobs will be to watch you, and if you even think about pointing your weapon toward our leader, they won't hesitate to shoot and kill you. They don't care that you don't have any ammunition in your weapons. They will kill you without hesitation. Don't be a stupid kid. I have seen it before, trust me, it's not pretty."

I believed him. I was sure this guy had a long, inter-esting story to tell, but for some reason, I had didn't want to hear about his bloody past.

Our training was short the day before the Army Pride Parade. They discharged us early, so we could rest up for the big day; however, we had to go back to school to collect the backpacks we'd left behind. My backpack was in the English class, and the room was crowded with other students trying to claim their belongings. I sat my Klakinshoof to the side, and I turned to talk to a kid I'd chatted with occasionally during training, both of us gathering our backpacks with our backs facing the rest of the room.

"How do you think it will go tomorrow?" my train-ing friend asked me.

"To be honest, I have no idea," I commented. "But one thing is for sure, we can't mess up."

"Wait!" I told my friend, as I turned back around. "Where is my Klakinshoof?"

"What? Are you serious?" My friend turned around abruptly, panic in his voice, but relief crossed his face when he saw that his Klakinshoof was still sitting there.

But mine had disappeared.

Dire scenarios flashed through my mind. Would I be the reason my dad spent the next fifteen years in prison. Or would I have to run away with my family? And if we ran, would they catch us and kill us all for treason?

My heart raced, and I was about to lose control of myself, but one thing I'd learned in these types of situations was to act smart. I examined the room quickly, and I noticed Salim, a kid I knew from last year's class, standing on the opposite side of the room. His smug grin struck me as an odd, made me think that he might have been the one who'd taken my weapon. So, I immediately knew that I had to put on a performance. I had to pretend that I already knew he had my Klakinshoof, and I just hoped he hadn't witnessed me a second ago discovering its loss and wondering aloud where it was.

I walked toward him and told Salim with a cool tone, "Okay, not funny, where did you put it? I need to leave, give it back, man."

Salim believed my act. He pulled my Klakinshoof from a behind a desk and said, "Too bad. I could have made a fortune off this."

It was an instant relief. I held my Klakinshoof

closely—as if it were a family member I'd been reunit-
ed with after many years. I caught my breath. It was
time to punish Salim for what he'd done.

I grabbed his collar and pushed him against the
rough, brick wall. "I will end your life if you ever try
something like this with me again."

He mumbled a few curse words as I stared him
down angrily. I wanted to beat the hell out of him,
and I came close, but a few other kids pulled me away
before I could.

∾

The next morning, it was time to don my
olive-colored soldier's uniform, my silly hat, and my
Klakinshoof. The outfit was way too big for me, and
I looked goofy in it, but my mom cried when she saw
me in it anyway.

"My outfit looks that bad, huh?" I was trying to
make her smile.

"I'm sorry, son, this is just wrong. What type of
monster thinks it's okay to give a child a weapon and
make him wear a soldier's uniform?" My mom continued crying. "You look so much like your uncle Mosa
in those clothes." I could see the fear in my mom's

eyes—the last time my uncle had worn this uniform, he hadn't come back.

"I'm not a child, mom. I will be okay," I responded, showing her nothing but strength. But inside me, there was nothing but fear. I was good at pretending now, good at hiding what my actual feelings were in order to make the people around me happy. It was sad, but it was the truth.

My mom handed me a hummus sandwich. "Here, take this with you."

"Mom, we're not allowed to carry any food."

"You have a big pocket. Hide it in there." She looked at me with wide, worried eyes and added, *"Please."*

"Okay. You're right. With this oversized outfit, no one would notice anyway." I laughed, pulling on the extra fabric to make my point.

"Do you want me to walk with you to the bus station?" my father offered.

"No, Dad, no need to."

Inside, I was screaming, *please, walk with me.* But I didn't want him to be involved in this.

My dad gripped my shoulder and pulled me close. "I will fix this, I promise, even if it means we have to leave the country. No kid your age should have to carry a weapon."

"You guys are being dramatic," I said, trying to ease their minds. "It's nothing but a parade. What could go wrong?" When I reached the threshold of the door, I turned and said, "All right, bye for now." And I walked out.

I took the bus to school, and as soon I arrived, I noticed there were around ten other buses and a few open-top trailers by the school's main door waiting to transport students to the parade.

"Some kids from Al-Kamalia will be joining us," one uniformed kid said to another as we waited to board the busses.

"Al-Kamalia was one of the worst municipalities in greater Baghdad area, a place where crime and poverty boomed. I'd been there before. They had mud-streets in the winter and a sand-streets in the summer. The government neglected the area, because the majority of the population were Shia Muslims, and although there were more Shia Muslims in Iraq than Sunni Muslims, Saddam Hussein was Sunni, and while technically secular, the Baath Party was largely considered Sunni as well. Shia and Sunni

Muslims occupied different branches of the Islamic family tree—they disagreed over doctrine and had been periodically at war for centuries. So, in the government-neglected, Shia-dominant Al-Kamalia municipality there were more cows and horses walking the streets than cars and people, and a trip there would have taken you back in time to the beginning of human civilization.

People there were not friendly either, and I believed neglect from the government had a lot to do with it. No power was ever provided to them. No clean water. No reliable public transportation. And a lack of these basic necessities had built into anger toward the outsiders.

My bus was number eight, and I would be sitting with the group I'd been training with, so it didn't matter to me if the new students behaved poorly.

We registered our names, and we stayed in line to hop on the bus, but when it was my turn, the instructor called me out, "Hey, you!"

"Yes, sir," I replied.

"Did you know the kid you helped the other day?"

I mumbled, "I don't know him personally, but I do remember him."

"Well, he killed himself!" The instructor sounded annoyed, not upset.

"Oh God, that is awful, Sir," I responded in shock.

"If you would have held your position instead of helping him, if you would have let me toughen him up, he would be living today, but you wanted to be a hero!"

I couldn't believe what he was saying. He was accusing me of causing a suicide, and I wanted it to tell him that maybe if he hadn't bullied and humiliated the kid in front of everyone, none of this would have ever happened. Maybe if the government hadn't decided to train underage kids how to use dangerous weapons, none of this would have ever happened. Maybe if the government had just let us be kids, none of this would have ever happened.

But again, I hid my actual feelings and pretended. "I'm deeply sorry, sir. I apologize for my arrogant act."

"Well, don't worry. I have the perfect punishment for you." He dragged me from my left shoulder, taking me in the direction of the open-top trailers.

I made sure hide my hummus sandwich, shutting my right pocket with my hand, so it wouldn't drop. I didn't want to give the instructor another excuse to abuse me. It turned out the open-top trailers were there to transport the students from Al-Kamalia, and the students were waiting in lines to board.

"Add his name to the list of trailer kids," the instructor said to the man in charge of the trailers.

"It is already packed with these animals," the guy in charge replied.

"I won't repeat myself again," the scar-faced guy insisted. He was determined to make me pay.

"Fine with me. I won't get into a fight with you over this. I can add another animal to the zoo."

He added my name to the list and demanded that I hop into the open-top trailer. Upon entering, the smell hit me so hard, I thought I'd fallen into a sewer. I couldn't bear it. The Al-Kamalia students—with their unwashed bodies, muddy shoes, and dirty uniforms—looked as if they'd just been released from an actual war. I wasn't sure if they'd ever taken a shower, but at least they hadn't for months. I could tell they'd been abused. They appeared as if they'd come from another world where civilization didn't exist yet, all of them mad and angry looking. I could sense the hate pouring from their eyes. Compared to these kids, I looked like royalty.

They ascertained from my clean outfit and non-smelly clothes, that I was meant to be on the bus, and they looked at me like I must have done something awful to have been abandoned here. I wanted them to keep thinking that way. I wanted them to believe I wasn't a good person. I couldn't show any weakness. I needed them to think I wasn't a good guy. It was the only way I could protect myself.

I took a corner in the trailer and said nothing. As I examined my environment, I noticed some guys staring at me already with crazed, curious eyes. I had to pretend I was a wild beast, so I started channeling Hareth's evil gaze.

One of the guys, who's hygiene was no better than a corpse's, said, "You must have done something nasty for them to shove you in here, Pretty Boy."

I responded, my voice practically a purr, "Yes, I convinced my friend to kill himself. Want to be next?" A maniacal grin spread across my face as I peered over at him.

The guy said no more. He believed I was crazy and left me alone.

After they locked the tailgate of the open-top trailers, there was nothing in there to see but sky and mean, angry guys.

So, this is what segregation feels like? I thought to myself.

In this case, we weren't segregated from the rest of the group because of the color of our skin, rather we were segregated based on religion. Everyone, besides me, in the trailer were Shia Muslims, and because Saddam Hussein and the government were Sunni, these people were nothing.

But I comforted myself. This problem existed everywhere in the world. Even in first world countries that claimed to have democracies, there were still groups of people suffering from discrimination. It was common—human nature, even. I wasn't sure why the thought was comforting, but it was. Maybe because if I convinced myself that evil was everywhere in the world, I would be able to make peace with my own situation and deal with my own problems without running away.

At 9 a.m., the trailer finally started moving. The bumpy road beneath us shook everyone left and right—maybe it was their way of making sure we would stay awake, alert, and ready for the parade.

For three hours we traveled, never knowing exactly where we were, and the trailer did not stop. Some people had already started throwing up, adding to the foul smell in the unbearably hot air. But I kept myself in check, still pretending to be strong.

It was noon, and I was starving. It was time to eat my hummus sandwich, but pulling it out in front of forty hungry kids was not a good idea. So, I decided to reach into my pocket and tear the sandwich into small pieces, hoping I would be able to eat each piece one at a time. That way, no one would catch onto what I was doing.

I managed to take two bites, but the kid beside me asked, "What are you eating?" Then he threatened, "Give me half of or I will tell everyone else."

I had no option but to share.

"Okay, but you will stand in front of me to hide what we're doing. I don't want anyone else to share this sandwich with us."

He was thinking, but I cut him off before he could come up with another plan.

"Do it now or I throw it over the open top, and no one will eat anything!" I needed him to know that I was in control.

He did what I asked, and we both ate the sandwich secretly without anyone noticing.

"Thank you," he said.

I raised an eyebrow at him, not sure if the words had really come from him.

He added, "I can tell you are a good person, and I can't wait for this to be over."

In that moment, he'd showed me his true self. He'd also been acting and pretending to be a tough guy, but I could see now that he was afraid as I was.

Some of the kids in this trailer might have been pretending to be vicious like me and this other kid. And some of the kids who were truly hard and angry inside, might have been different had it not been for the circumstances of their lives that had forced them to become something they were not. It didn't excuse immoral acts, but I knew that evil was man-made, knew that it was a creation of a society.

By 3 p.m., we'd all started losing our patience, had all started revealing our demons. I was losing my patience too and I was hungry, but at least I'd been able to eat half a sandwich to fuel my strength.

Everyone started acting like the caged animals that they wanted us to be. Some kids tried to jump out of the moving trailer, others started fighting with each other. But the worst incident was when some kids tried to abuse a weaker kid sexually. He was skinny and pale, and he seemed relatively cleaner than the other kids who started pushing him around. When he stopped fighting back, they held him down as they tried to rape him. It became so crowded around him, that I never saw exactly what they did to him, but I wasn't able to help. I wanted so badly to use my weapon to stop them, but I didn't have any bullets, and I was sure if I tried to save him, I would be the next victim.

By 5 p.m., eight hours into our ordeal, I'd started losing my mind. The trailer was still moving but slowly.

"How we are not running out of gas?" some kids were questioning aloud.

"When we are going to get there?" other kids were shouting, hoping the driver would acknowledge them.

"I wish this damn truck would break down or something, so I can climb up and leave," another kid said.

"You don't want to run away, trust me," a kid far away from me responded.

"Yes, get rid of that the idea, Pal," the guy who I'd shared my food with responded to the kid. "The punishment would be a million times worse. Running away would be considered betraying your country— you would get jail time, and so would your father."

I would rather have died in that trailer than have been the reason my father saw jail time. I needed to suck it up. I told myself everyone was living in this shit-hole of a world, and I wasn't the only one.

The walls of the trailer were covered in hot, smelly pee, some of it my own pee because I had no other option. They would not let us out. At 7 p.m., when we finally stopped, some kids climbed the pee-covered walls of the trailer to see what was happening, and to see if they were finally going to release us for the parade. They were like a bunch of pirates in the movies who'd been at sea so long, they were checking the horizon for land.

"Damn it," one of the pirate kids announced. "We're not there yet. We've only stopped to refuel."

My head lowered in defeat. "Where are we now, anyway?" I asked the kid, hoping he would have an answer.

"I have no idea, but I think we are still far from where we should be."

"Hey, get down from there, before I shoot you

down!" the instructor yelled from outside the trailer.

"Please, Sir," the kid begged "We are hungry. Many of us have already fainted in here. We need some food. Please help us out."

"I will see what I can do, get back down," the instructor said.

Other kids inside the trailer started shouting, "Please, sir, we are hungry! Please, sir, we are hungry!"

The words did not sound angry or violent, only weak and afraid—just like normal kids. Oddly, maybe even shamefully, I was relieved. With all the other kids revealing that they were just as week as me—I didn't have to worry about them hurting me, not right then.

We all repeatedly chanted, "We are hungry! We are hungry!"

Finally, the instructor started throwing dry, cold bread in bags over the top of the open trailer. All the kids rushed to hijack a piece, and in some cases, we stepped on each other. I was lucky enough that one of the bags hit me directly in the chest, and all the bread inside scattered across the floor at my feet. I held one piece with an angry face, a warning for everyone else to stay back.

The bread rain stopped, and all of us had claimed a piece except for the kid who'd been abused earlier. Everyone was busy eating their cold, dry bread, so it was my chance to approach him without being noticed. As I stepped closer to the abused kid, but he retreated, terrified of me.

"Stay away from me," he told me, his eyes facing the ground.

"It's okay. Don't worry. I won't hurt you," I told him, removing my fake evil expression. I went on, "Sorry for what happened to you earlier. Take half of my bread."

He stared at me, surprised, as if he'd never been treated with respect before. He hesitated to reach for the bread, so I reached for his hand and put the bread in his palm. "Eat. You'll need it, trust me. We don't know when we'll arrive, and you don't want to faint from hunger. You know the punishment for people who fail."

He nodded, tears slipping down his cheeks as he started eating. "Can you stay next to me?"

I'd had terrible experiences with trying to protect or defend weaker kids in my life, and I'd paid significantly for it before. Anmar crossed my mind for a second and the beating I'd taken for standing up for him. Samy crossed my mind too. I'd ended up in this trailer, because I'd had the nerve to help him after he'd fainted.

But I decided I couldn't change who I was, nor could I change who my parents had raised me to be, so I responded with a smile and confidence, "Sure, I will. I won't let anyone harm you. Plus, I won't hesitate to put the spear of my Klakinshoof up someone's ass if they try to."

We chuckled, and I guarded the kid until our arrival at the Army Pride Parade.

We arrived two hours later, at 9 p.m.

When the trailer door finally opened, voices out in the dark yelled, "Yalla! Yalla!" *Let's go. Let's go.*

We rushed out, gasping in freedom of the night air, but someone held my arm back. I turned. It was the kid I'd shared my bread with.

"Thank you," he said.

I nodded and moved on.

In this new group, I wasn't sure where my position would be. I registered my name again with the new instructor to make sure my father or I wouldn't receive any punishment for betraying our country. I stood by the kid who'd forced me to share my sandwich with him, and we started marching to Army Pride Parade.

The instructor yelled at us, "You walk as one! You turn as one! Keep your chests high and your weapons stable—unshakable! Represent your country well! Today you get the honor of seeing our great leader!"

He was preparing us just as we were about to hit the cameras and the media. We continued our march, and finally, we turned right, and there was Saddam Hussein, waving his right hand, proud of his bogus army.

I had so many questions I wanted to ask him, but his snipers would have put a bullet through my head if I'd moved one foot out of line. I wondered whether he was aware that we were just school kids forced to march in his parade. I wondered whether he was aware that we were all hungry, wondered whether he was aware that we'd been locked in a trailer for an entire day, and now we had to pretend we were his army. I wondered whether he was aware that his people didn't have reliable electricity or water, that we didn't have enough food. I wondered whether he was aware that religious discrimination was tearing his country apart. He was standing tall, confident. And he seemed powerful enough to conquer the world if he wanted to. But then I wondered if he was also pretending. Maybe he was a good person? He just didn't know the truth.

The five-minute march was over. I'd finished playing my part in Saddam's army of illusion. We'd been locked in a trailer for fourteen hours for this! But it was finally over.

Jon: I want you to smile. This was not the worst thing that ever happened to me.

CHAPTER
Sixteen

Completion of the Soul

Baghdad, late 1999
Adam: fifteen years old

Jon, when we first meet in high school, your Western name told me you were Christian, so I approached you. I still recall the first conversation we ever had ...

"Hey, I haven't seen you before. What school did you come from?" I asked.

"I'm from Karada," you said. "My family moved here in the summer." They hadn't. You'd moved to live with your grandparents, but you didn't tell me that at the time.

I took in your expensive looking shoes and gathered that you came from a wealthy family. "Oh, cool I hope you like it here."

"I hope so, too, what's your name?"

"Adam"

"Are you going to be in my class, Adam?" you asked.

I said, "I think so, since you're standing here."

We both started laughing for no reason.

I wanted to know more about you. I wondered if you'd suffered from religious discrimination, too, since you were a Christian like me. And you had.

We become friends quickly, and after a few months you became a big part of my life. Throughout the following eighteen years and counting, you and I have continued to be bonded as soul brothers. And you always signed birthday cards to me with these words: *To my forever friend, I wish you a happy birthday! Regards! Your soul's completion.*

~

"My grandparents kicked me out," you once told me while standing in front of my apartment building.

"What? What happened? Come in," I said to you.

And as usual, when any friends came over to our house, my mom greeted you and started asking how your parents were doing, even though she'd never meet them.

"They are doing good thanks, Ante," you lied—you didn't even live with your parents. "How are you doing?"

"Fine, thank you, son," she said. "Would you like me to fix you both some tea?"

I wanted my mom to leave already, so I could find out what had happened to you.

"We're good, Mom," I told her. "We're leaving soon anyway."

I took you to our balcony where we kept wooden chairs to sit in.

"That bitch, Karema," you started explaining before we'd even sat down.

"Who?" I asked. For a second, I'd forgotten who she was.

"My uncle's wife!" You shot me a look that said, *what the hell?*

"Oh, sorry, yeah, Karema. What did she do?"

"She kept nagging my grandmother and uncle about how I shouldn't be living there, kept telling them I should respect my parents and go back home to Karada to live with them." Your eyebrows had pulled together, and anger was pouring from your wide, hazel eyes. Then you added, "And today I caught her saying the same thing again, so I yelled at her. I told her that this was my grandparents' house, not hers, so maybe *she* should leave."

"Oh shit, you didn't." I knew what kind of trouble you would of be in. Your uncle would not let that fly.

"And your uncle kicked you out?" I asked.

You nodded your head and added, "What bothered me most was that my grandmother agreed with them." Your face was red. "My uncle's wife has so many rules and is always criticizing everything I do, even if I go straight to my room and mind my own business. But even she is better than going back home to my parent's house. But now I don't have a choice, they all want me to go back home where I'll receive all that abuse again from my father and my oldest brother. Did they forget why I was with them in the first place? Did they forget how my dad knocked me down so hard that my head started bleeding, all for not letting my brother use my towel?" Unshed tears were glistening in your eyes. "I will run away, and no one will know where I am."

You were never certain of your future. You weren't entirely happy, even at your grandparent's house. And you never felt entirely wanted. So, every time you weren't pleased with your circumstances, you rebelled and made the most dangerous decision possible in the name of trying to improve your situation.

"Okay," I said. "Don't make a decision like that while you're angry. How many times do I have to tell you?" I put a hand on your shoulder. "Why don't you stay with me for few days, until the things calm down a bit?" I put the invitation out there, but I knew you would never accept, so I changed tactics. "Why don't you call your mom and tell her you're coming home? You know she would be happy."

I knew you missed your mom a lot. You didn't speak about her much, but when you did your eyes lit up with happiness.

You turned to look at me. "What about my dad and my stupid brother?"

"Try to avoid them. I mean, you guys have your own rooms. When they are at home, stay in your room. They won't notice." I hated trying to convince you to leave, when that meant I wouldn't get to see you as much, but I wanted what was best for you. I only wished I was certain that returning to your parent's house *was* what was best for you.

You finally agreed, and you went back to your

parents' house, but it was only for a few weeks, and you ran away from them again. Thankfully, you were allowed to return to your grandparents' house.

You had a tough life in ways that I didn't, but I was always by your side, ready to walk miles with you if I had to.

In the next year, we met another kid in high school—James. He had a Western name like yours, so we knew he was a Christian. Most of the Christian kids in Iraq had Western names, but my siblings and I were exceptions to the rule. But unlike my siblings' names, Adam was an Arabic name as well as a Christian one—my father had been smart enough to have chosen a name that pleased everyone, one he'd hoped would prevent me from getting harassed at school, too bad it didn't work.

James' friendship was a shock to my system. After a few conversations, we hated each other. We disagreed about everything, and it was difficult to know what he would do next, which left me uneasy around him.

While we were sitting in the class one day, waiting for our math teacher to show up, James entered the room by kicking the door open with his foot.

"Another shitty day at school," he was already

complaining before class had even started. He looked over at us. "What are you girls gossiping about this early?" He landed in a chair, laughing at his own joke.

"Talking about your hot mom," you said.

I couldn't help it. I laughed.

"You guys are some silly shit," James said as he started drawing with a marker on the desk.

"You know that's Ahmed's desk, and he will kick your ass for doing that," I said.

Students said Ahmed had OCD, since he liked everything around him to be clean.

"Let him try," James said, sounding confident, arrogant even.

In the span of several minutes, the desk had already been ruined by James' crazy drawings and the random letters that he'd written, so what else could I even do?

James said to you, "Your Jeans?"

"What about them?" you replied.

"Did you buy them in Karada?" James was still drawing at the desk, not making eye contact with you.

"Yes," you responded. "They're comfortable. I love the style of these jeans."

"I don't know about that. That style was from two years ago. In fact, I had the same kind. I believe my mom started using it to clean the floors."

James' words shocked me. *What an asshole!* I thought to myself.

But as the year went on, we learned that James was just like that sometimes. He would say anything to annoy you or get a rise out of you.

For some reason, we'd argue with James for hours, and yet, he would still talk to both of us the next day as if nothing had happened. It was an interesting relationship, but I needed someone blunt like him. He never hesitated to tell me the truth. After one year, I could not live without James' bluntness either—he balanced out my soul and became the completion of it, just like you.

Jon: I want you to smile. Your friendship and James' friendship were two of the best things that ever happened to me.

CHAPTER
Seventeen

English Teacher

Baghdad, late 1999 (early in the new school year)
Adam: fifteen years old

His name was Samer Hani—a tall, dark, not-in-shape guy, with an exotropia eye condition but the confidence of a world leader. He was an English teacher, and he was better than a video game at claiming my attention. He chose his words wisely and acted respectfully. He used Shakespeare's *The Merchant of Venice* to teach us English.

His lectures were compelling. I ended up knowing the play by heart. Although I'd started my English lessons at eleven years old and it was the third language I'd learned, everything about English sounded interesting.

As Mr. Hani once said, "The language is simple, direct, and has and no hidden meanings." At least, that was what he believed.

It was remarkable how he was able to describe the characters in the play with such passion. He gave us the impression that he lived with these characters, and they were like his family.

"The greedy Shylock demanded a pound of Antonio's flesh as collateral against a loan he provided him," Mr. Hani explained to us. "Antonio wanted to help his best friend, Bassanio, even though it could cost him his life. What a beautiful world it would be if we loved each other as much as these two friends did? No war, no hate, only love and honesty."

When I noticed antisemitic undertones in the play, I was upset. I didn't like that Shakespeare associated the evil character, Shylock, with Judaism. But I knew Mr. Hani hadn't chosen the play. Rather, everything he taught, was selected by the government, and he did his best to focus on the good parts of the story, ignoring the negative writings that promoted hate. In fact, he never once mentioned to us that Shylock was Jewish, completely ignoring that specific fact in the book.

"You, my dear student," Mr. Hani said to me.

"Yes, Mr. Hani," I answered.

"What is your name?" he asked me.

"Adam," I told him using a firm voice, so I wouldn't have to repeat myself.

"Oh, Adam, yes. I know your dad. He told me to be expecting you this year." Mr. Hani smiled. "He is my barber."

I smiled back without saying anything. The comment was common—a lot of older people got their hair cut at my dad's shop.

Mr. Hani asked me politely again, "Can you please read act four, scene one for the class?"

I began reciting it in a British accent as he'd taught us in class.

He was impressed with my performance. "Well done," he said, clapping his hands. "That is what I call a clean read—confident and from the heart! I hope the rest of you will learn from Adam's example today." Mr. Samer smiled, his voice rising. "I will call you, Prince! A clean voice with such confidence must be called *The Prince of the Class*. You deserve it."

For the rest of the week, he demanded that everyone in the class to call me "Prince" as long he was present. I smiled. It was a good feeling.

James, who sat behind me, whispered under his breath, "Dude! Are you sure he isn't a pedophile? You may want to watch your butt around him."

You laughed, *Jon.*

I turned my head towards you and made a crude gesture. "Give me a break you guys. I can't get a compliment without you guys being annoying assholes."

You guys laughed at me, until Mr. Samer, with his exotropia eye, gave us all a firm stare, and we shut our mouths immediately.

Mr. Hani had a great approach to teaching. He made sure his students felt their achievements, and because I was *over*-rewarded for my efforts, I continued to work harder in order to taste more success. I wanted more. By the end of the year, I'd kept my Prince title, and I'd managed to make the highest score in the class.

Jon: I want you to smile. This was one of the good things that happened to me in Iraq.

CHAPTER
Eighteen

The Third and Fourth Separation

Baghdad, 2000
Adam: sixteen years old

Two years later and the conversation between Nabeel and my father had flip-flopped. My father told Nabeel he had to leave.

"What about you guys? Why can't we leave all at once?" Nabeel asked.

"You need to listen to me. We've survived too many wars already. We can't continue to test our luck. In one night of bombings, we nearly lost Adam, and we could have lost all of you. Then, your fifteen-year-old brother was conscripted into weapons training at school and transported in a trailer for twelve hours to participate in the Army Pride Parade. Not to mention,

I don't know how much longer earning your master's degree will protect you, besides you don't have much time left anyway. I must at least try to save some of you, and right now, you're the one most at risk. I already called Lena. She promised she would send money to support you in Jordan. I will bring you a passport by Friday, and I want you to leave on Saturday."

"In two days?" Nabeel's eyes were wide with shock. "I won't have a chance to say goodbye to all my friends. I was probably wrong, Dad. Maybe I should just stay with you guys."

Nabeel had changed his mind over the past two years, or maybe he hadn't been all that convicted to go in the first place. He'd always been more attached to the family than Amar, and he was the trying to find any excuse to stay now.

My dad responded, "You can write letters, son. Trust me. This is your last chance. When this winter break from school is over, you won't have another chance to leave Iraq forever! Nothing can hold you back. Not your friends, not even your own family."

My dad had chosen winter break for Nabeel to leave, so it would be less suspicious when he requested the passport from the government. It would only be valid for the winter break, just enough time for a vacation in Jordan.

My mom was hopeless. She didn't like it, but she agreed with my dad. She couldn't change anything, and there were no other options. "Listen to your dad," my mom said. "Take the chance son and find a better life. There is no more future for you here."

My parents proceed with the plan. My father booked everything, and my mom prepared Nabeel's bags, loading them with clothes that would keep him warm and a week's worth of rice, dates, and her hand-made Koleja—a pastry Nabeel loved.

On Saturday at 1 p.m., my father said the same words he did when Amar was leaving, "It's time, Nabeel, we need to leave. Say goodbye to everyone!"

This was the third separation we'd endured as family, first Lena and Amar and now Nabeel.

We should be used to this by now, I told myself.

The sadness was the same. The feeling was the same. I was losing another brother. He wasn't dying. He was going so that he could live, but I wouldn't know for sure whether I would ever see him again, the same way I wasn't sure if I would ever see Amar or Lena again.

They'd left, and now I only ever saw them in pictures.

Will I ever see them again? I asked myself as Nabeel came toward me for a hug goodbye.

"Don't do anything crazy, Adam," Nabeel whispered in my ear as he hugged me. Then he moved on to hug Rami and my sisters.

At this point, everyone was crying, but my mom was sobbing, choking on her tears, and I wasn't sure whether anyone would ever be able to stop it.

Nabeel cracked a joke to calm her down. "Don't worry, Mom, with all the rice and dates you put in my bag, I will survive for at least another two years." He hugged her and kissed her forehead.

We laughed and cried at the same time, and he walked away.

Leaving Iraq is the only way for him to survive, I told myself, as he walked out the main door and disappeared.

Our rotary-dial, home phone rang at midnight. No one called at that hour, except my sister, Lena.

"Hello? Hello? Mom, can you hear me?" Lena said on the other end of the phone.

The connection was bad, but I still replied. "It's me, Adam, how are you, Lena?"

My parents rushed to the phone, my mother snatching the phone from my hand as she gushed, "Lena, my love. I've missed you. How are you doing?" Tears were on her cheeks already. A few seconds passed and my mom told us, "She says she has good news!" Then she said to Lena over the phone, "Lena, hearing your voice and knowing you are doing well is the best news I could ask for." My mom meant every word.

My dad tried to steal the phone from my mom, but she held on tight. It was funny seeing them grappling over it like that.

Finally, my father succeeded in stealing the phone. "Lena, baby, how are you?" And he asked another ten questions all at the same time.

"Let her respond," my mom punched him lightly on his shoulder. They both now had their ears pressed against the receiver.

"I'm doing good, Dad," I caught her saying. "Before my card minutes are over, I want to tell you some happy news."

"Go ahead, baby, what it is?" my dad responded.

She answered on the other end, but I couldn't hear her clearly this time.

"No. I don't recall. What application?" my father

said, a confused frown on his face. He looked at my mom. "Do you recall her putting in an application for all of us?"

"Eight years ago, Putrus," my mom whispered, her hand over the phone receiver, so if anyone were listening no one would be able to hear. "Don't you remember? She put in an application for visas, so we could go over and live with her."

"Oh, yeah, what about it? Did we all get accepted?" My dad laughed, thinking it was a joke.

My mom put a hand over her mouth, stunned. She looked at me and relayed Lena's message. "It *was* accepted, but not for all of us, only for me and your dad. Our applications are in the final stage of the process. She says your dad and I can come over, but all of you would have to wait a few more years."

My dad was silent. And after she'd relayed the message, my mom was too. Suddenly, they'd stopped fighting for the phone. They weren't sure whether to be happy or sad. They could leave, but what good did that do if most of their kids were still here?

"Dad, are you still there? Hello? Hello?" I heard my sister say through the phone. My dad was holding it by his side.

"Yes, Lena, we're here," he said "So, none of your siblings have been accepted?"

After a moment, my dad was the one to relay her message this time. "She says no, unfortunately, they'll have to wait two more years. She's telling me that your mom and I can come over, and she's trying to convince me that Rana can take care of you kids, while we work to support you from there. Since we'd be able to earn so much more, she says we'd be able to help Nabeel and Amar too."

Lena never said over the phone where she lived, though her calls came in from the United States. And when talking to her, my parents only referred to the place she lived as "her city."

My mom took the phone from my dad. "Lena!" She shouted her name. "Proceed with your dad's application. He is coming as soon as you can finish his paperwork. I will stay here with kids until their applications are approved."

"What? No! I'm not going anywhere without you or the kids! You go!" My dad was annoyed.

My mom gestured her disagreement, making a shooing motion with her hand. "Nabeel and the kids need you to be there, not here. Your barbershop barely covers our meals."

Rana, who was standing to my left, gave my mom a look that said not discuss our living conditions on the phone. It was also a reminder that the government could be listening.

My mom nodded, signaling to Rana that she would say no more. "Yes, Lena. We can't say much right now, but please proceed as I told you. Your dad and I will call you later, okay, baby. Love you!"

My mom did not receive any response. She held the phone away from her face and looked at it. Lena's card minutes must have been out, and the call had already been disconnected.

My mom addressed my dad after she hung up the phone. "You can't be serious about rejecting this opportunity again."

I wasn't aware my father had had such an opportunity before.

But my mom went on, her voice angry, "If you'd listened to me back in 1989, we would all be living in Athens, and we wouldn't have gone through any of this. Agree with me for once!"

"Is this true?" Rana asked. "Did we really have a chance to leave Iraq before?"

Rana and I learned that the answer was yes, and then we proceeded to the living room by ourselves. Our mom had never mentioned it before, because she hadn't wanted our dad to blame himself for everything we'd gone through. But their debate raged on now in the kitchen.

"So, Mom is using this information to force him to agree?" I asked Rana.

"I believe that is Mom's plan," Rana answered.

"What about Sam?" I asked Rana. Sam was a teacher who preached at the same church Rana went to, and he'd proposed to her a month ago.

"What about him?" she said.

"If Dad leaves, are you going to postpone your marriage?"

Before Rana could respond, we heard our dad tell our mom, "Well, I want to attend Rana's wedding. I can't just leave."

Rana's wedding was scheduled for August, and everything had already been booked. It would have been hard, if not impossible, to change the date. She would have lost her deposit for the banquet hall.

My mom assured my dad, "You will attend the wedding, but you have to do what needs to be done after the wedding." She held his shoulder and added, "Trust me on this. It's for you and your kids' benefit."

Patiently, we all waited for the wedding day. Our feelings were mixed. We weren't sure if we desperately wanted to see Rana be married or we wanted the wedding to be over with, so my dad could go to America and support us, so he could begin a journey towards a better life. I believed both feelings were valid. As was the dread—because we didn't want to see our dad go.

Finally, it was August 8th, the day Rana—a beautiful, white dove in her dress—would be married. She wore a simple, white necklace, and a white veil that partially covered her face, but I could still see her almond-shaped eyes filled with happiness.

Rana's maid of honor was my sister Reem. She wore long, blush-pink dress with a high neck, and her makeup perfectly complemented her dress color, creating a vision of beauty the likes of which I'd only ever see on TV.

It was a simple wedding. Sam was able to rent a banquet hall and buy a seven-layer cake, and every guest received one can of Pepsi. But unfortunately, they could not afford to provide dinner for all the guests, so it was a wedding without dinner. But it didn't stop them from being the happiest couple on Earth—then, and for the following seventeen years and counting. It was hard to find a relationship like theirs.

Rana moved out of our house after the wedding. She started living in a small room in her mother-in-law's house. It wasn't as traumatic as when Amar or Nabeel had left. She was fifteen minutes from our apartment. She visited every weekend, never missing one.

The day after the wedding, my mom asked my dad, "Please proceed now with the passport."

My dad was not at all happy with the plan. But at this point, he had no options. He had two kids already wandering around the world, desperate and with no definite future. And four more of his kids were still suffering here. My dad had to do it to save us. Maybe we could settle in Michigan with Lena and be safe.

Even though it was close to impossible to get any legal documents from the governments without paying a bribe, my dad was able to receive his passport with less difficulty than my brothers, because he was too old to serve in the army.

As my father was preparing his luggage the day before his planned departure date, my mom, Rana, and Reem were helping him.

"I don't think I can do this," Reem said and started crying.

"Don't let your dad see you. It would break his heart," my mom said.

As Rana folded our father's clothes, I could see her eyes glistening with tears too, but she pretended they were not there.

I did as Rana did and pretended it did not affect me, but inside, I was torn apart.

The next day I held back my tears when the car came to pick up my dad. I was not sure if I would ever see me again, and I wanted to be sure that a crying face was not the last thing he remembered about me. Unfortunately, no one else was able to do the same. They were all crying.

My mom finally told my dad, "I'm sorry, you know what, maybe we shouldn't do this. I was selfish to put you in this position."

My mom's tears could shake the core of even the hardest human beings. But I didn't shed a single tear.

My dad hugged my mom. "You were never selfish.

We need to do what is good for our kids. This is not the end. We will see each other again."

My father said those words, but we all knew nothing was for sure in Iraq. There was a possibility that we would never see each other again. But we had experience goodbyes before. We were aware what it truly meant.

Reem, who was eighteen at the time, cried hysterically.

My dad said, "Stop it, baby. I will be back! I will be back! I promise I will be back!" He repeated himself, but she did not show any sign that she believed him. He hugged her.

She was nearly choking from crying, but she didn't say anything.

My father could not take it anymore. He kissed her and walked away—no turning back. I helped carry his luggage downstairs, managing to hold back my tears successfully. The only feeling I let show was my faked strength. I wanted to leave him with the message that I'd protect his family, despite how young I was and despite however long we'd be parted.

We loaded his luggage, and he hugged me. "Take care of your sisters and brother, okay?" He held both shoulders and shook me. He was seeking emotions from me, but I did not show any.

With an expressionless face, I replied, "Don't worry, Dad. I will protect them. No harm will come to any of them." My tone was robotic but firm. I sounded the way I had as I'd prepared for the Army Pride Parade—like I was pretending.

He kissed my forehead. "Goodbye, son!" He got in the SUV, and the car drove away.

When it turned left by the end of the street, I walked over to the stairs of the apartment building, making sure no one was around as I dropped to my knees and released all the sadness I'd kept pent up for the past few days. I sobbed until there were no more tears to shed, then I wiped my face and walked back to my apartment, pretending my dad's departure hadn't affect me at all.

I showed my family nothing but strength.

Jon: I want you to smile. This was not the worst thing that ever happened to me.

CHAPTER
Nineteen

The Result: 99.96%

Baghdad, 2002
Adam: eighteen years old

Rami took the responsibility of the barbershop. I was helping him at least one shift a day, but I refused to be a barber—there was nothing I hated more than cutting or cleaning a strangers' hair. I insisted on keeping my distance from customers, but I helped clean the shop and clean the supplies, helped keep the shop presentable for customers. We were both going to school—Rami in his second year of college and me in my last year of high school—as we took full responsibility for working in my dad's absence. Our poorer grades started to show, but my mom didn't give us a hard time. She was aware that it wasn't easy for us to do both. She let it go, as long as we passed our classes—which we had to do in order to put off our army service. Thankfully, even with my extra work and divided attention, my former status as an excellent student only dropped down to that of a decent student, and it was still enough to keep me on track for college.

My family agreed that if anyone asked us where my dad was, we would tell them my uncle was having heart surgery in Jordan, and my dad needed to be with him for at least a year. I didn't know if everyone believed us, but we had to tell them something. I couldn't trust anyone—except you and James. They were aware of every detail in my life, so I couldn't hide the truth from them.

On an early Friday morning, we were waiting for Rana to show up. She had a baby girl named Nena and a baby boy named Fares now, and they were all going to spend the day and night at our house.

The doorbell rang, but no one moved.

"God, you guys are so lazy," I complained. "Can't anyone get up to open the door?" I headed outside through the balcony to open the main door. The doorbell rang again. "I'm coming, Rana. Be patient!"

I opened the door to find a short, skinny guy with a

shaved head, wearing a suit without a tie. He was pale, and the suit did not fit him properly—half of his hand was covered by his sleeves. He greeted me in Arabic.

I responded with the same greeting, also speaking in Arabic, then I added, "How can I help you, sir?"

"I know your dad. He is a dear friend of mine."

"Oh, okay," I said. "I'm sorry. Have we met? What is your name?"

"Abu Sami," he responded. And switching from Arabic to Aramaic he said, "He told me he was going to America, and I was so happy for him!"

He was lying. My father told us when he was leaving that he'd told no one where he was going, and he had warned us to be careful of someone trying to trick us into admitting where he really was. Normally, in Iraq, we didn't let guests stand in the doorway for more than a minute—it was considered rude. But I didn't trust this guy, and he didn't know that my dad had prepared me for a situation like this one.

I responded, feigning shock, "What? What are you talking about? Is my father lying to us? What are you saying?"

The guy looked at me, confused. My acting was perfect!

I continued my performance. "Please, sir, tell me the truth, is he cheating on my mom? I won't tell her, but I must know the truth. He told us he was going to Jordan, because my uncle is having heart surgery."

The guy didn't know what to say. "I'm sorry I don't know why I said America. Yes, he told me Jordan. I hope your uncle is well."

I faked relief, then I added, "I was going to say, sir, my dad is not that type of person."

"No, he is not. I wanted to swing by to see if you guys need anything while your dad is away."

"I appreciate you, sir. We are doing fine. Oh, how rude of me, would you like to come in?" I didn't want to give him reason to be suspicious about anything.

He responded, "That's all right. I need to get going. Thank you anyway." He turned and walked away. I had a feeling he was sent by the government to trick me into admitting my dad was in the United States. I did my best to confuse him and make him believe my story.

My mom yelled, "Adam, who is it?"

I shut the door. "No one. Wrong address." I stood behind a cement pole on the balcony, hiding as I watched the guy walk away from our building. I waited to see if he would turn and look back. I told myself if he turned, it meant he didn't buy my story, and he wanted to know if I was watching him. But luckily, he didn't turn. He'd bought in my story. He was walking with quick steps as if he needed to be somewhere else.

"Mom, I will be back," I shouted. It wasn't the smartest thing, but I went downstairs and followed the guy, keeping a good distance. I wanted to confirm that he was from the government. Sure enough, after fifteen minutes, he entered a government security building.

I went back home and told my family everything. I also warned them that they might make more attempts to find out information. "We must stick to the same story," I told my family, and they all agreed.

While we were discussing the possibility that the government had become suspicious of my father's absence, it was announced on TV that Saddam Hussein would allow the public to vote.

We all turned towards the TV, not believing what we'd just heard.

"What?" Reem said. "This has got to be a joke."

I started laughing. I couldn't hold it in.

"Have you lost your minds?" my mom whisper-yelled and Reem and me. "The walls have ears. Shut your mouths."

"You think there will be any opponents?" Rami asked.

Sam was over at my house as well, and he didn't seem as shocked as everyone else. He'd known this was coming. He worked as a teacher, but he had close friends in the Baath party. They trusted him enough to have told him what was going on.

"He will have no opponents," Sam said. "The people will simply vote yes or no to the question of whether or not they want him to be in power for the next seven years."

"Is this a joke?" I asked Sam, echoing Reem's earlier sentiment.

He ignored me.

"Do you think people will vote?" Rami asked.

Sam was serious. "Don't joke about it. This is a housecleaning, not a vote. They're looking to eliminate anyone who still has a rebel spirit."

A few days later, we received ballots with everyone's names on them. But there was a problem—we'd still received ballots for my dad, Nabeel, and Amar, and they would not be here to vote. My mom and I were a little worried about what would happen if they didn't show up. Would their absences bring further scrutiny from the government?

My mom called Rana. "I need you and Sam to come over. I need to talk to you both." Rana said something on the other end of the line, before my mom added, "Yes. Everything is fine. We just need to talk."

At my mom's request, Rana and her husband showed up at 5 p.m. "What's wrong?" Rana asked before she stepped inside the house.

"Sit down. I told you everything is fine. I just have a question. Do you want something to drink?" My mom was not acting stressed.

Rana's face was puzzled. "Tea is fine."

After my mom placed the teapot on the stove, she placed the ballots on the table.

Rana glanced at them and said, "Oh, that!"

My mom said, "Yes, so, do you think it will be a problem?" She fixed her eyes on Sam. "What do you think? We need any intel you have."

Sam was annoyed by the intel comment—people could be executed for even talking the wrong way.

He responded with a calm tone. "The government

is requiring only one representative from each household. If you don't overreact, they won't be suspicious." He told us that we had to vote yes—there would be grave consequences if we voted no.

"Well, good," my mom said. "I don't need to panic. Sorry, I couldn't ask this question over the phone."

"No worries, Mom. I needed a break," Rana said.

My mom turned to me. "Adam, can you please fill them out and take them to our polling location. It's going to be at your old elementary school."

My memories of that place were not great. I grabbed one of the ballots, and I examined it. There were only a few words—the name of the voter, one question, and two options.

Do you want our current leader, Saddam Hussein, to serve as Iraq's leader for the next seven years?

I stared at the two boxes with the options. I strongly wanted to select no. I even asked myself, *What's the worst that could happen?*

Saddam had asked the citizens of this country to answer a question. Why were we all too weak to answer the way we wanted to? Maybe Saddam actually wanted to know the truth. I picked yes for all my siblings—for the ones who lived with me and for the ones all over the world. I selected yes for my father as well.

But when it came time to make my own selection, I toyed with the idea of selecting no for a few minutes.

I'd nearly pressed my pen on the box for "no," when Rana said, "Did you finish?"

I lifted my pen, leaving the box empty. "Yes, I have. I'll take them tomorrow." I shoved my ballot in with the others, and I set it on the table for the next day.

In the morning, the TV was filled with songs about Saddam Hussein, songs about how we would sacrifice ourselves for him, because he was the savior of our country, songs about how he'd been able to defeat the whole world with his army. At this point, everyone in Iraq knew everything they saw and heard on TV was a lie.

I ignored the TV. "Mom, I'm going to head down to the polling location, then I will meet up with Rami at the barbershop."

"Okay, love. Take care of yourself," my mom replied to me from the kitchen, the same way she did on any normal day.

I started walking toward my old school, recalling all the terrible memories I'd experienced in the old building. The loss of my friendship with Anmar. The beating I'd taken from Hareth and his friends. The beatings I'd received from teachers and all the other abuses I'd suffered at the school. This place had shaped me into the person I was today. It *had* made me tough, but I hadn't let it turn me into an angry person, hadn't let it fill me with hate. It wasn't easy to walk by the spot where I'd once been beaten and dragged by my cross-chain, but I arrived at our polling place anyway.

There were ten polling boxes and many people standing in line. After waiting for about fifteen minutes, it was my turn to drop our ballots in the box. I reached out to the box, but the attendant snatched my hand before I could drop the papers in.

"How old are you?" he asked.

"Eighteen," I responded.

"Let me see what you have there." The attendant pulled the ballots out of my hand without waiting for me to give them to him.

Oh God, did I mark my ballot no? I left it blank, right? My palms started sweating, my heart racing and my mind swirling. Was this damn building cursed? Every time I was here, I landed in trouble. But this mistake could cost me my life—why had I been so stupid? My mind wouldn't quit.

The poll attendant went through the ballots, and he stopped on the last one, grimacing. "What is this?" He shook the paper in my face. "Are you deaf? What is this?" He insisted I answer his question.

I mumbled, "What is it, sir?"

He showed me my poll.

I turned my head to glance at the ballot, and thank god, it was still blank. I didn't want to answer the man, but I had to. "Oh God, I'm sorry I must have missed the last one. As you can see, all the others are marked yes. I'm not sure how I missed that one."

He replied, "Okay, mark your vote!" He handed me a pen.

I marked it yes. He took the poll from my hand, checked it again, and dropped it in the box.

As he was doing that, a young man from the other side of the boxes yelled, "NO, please! Please! I didn't mean to. It was a mistake!"

The attendant and I both turned toward the begging voice.

The young guy was around my age, and two guys in government uniforms were dragging him through the sand, kicking him and shouting, "Traders like yourself don't deserve this country!"

People were whispering around me.

"What's wrong?" someone asked.

"He voted no," another answered.

It could have been me! I thought to myself. If Rana hadn't interrupted me last night, I would have selected no. I walked away, my head reeling, helplessly watching as this young man took a beating because he'd voted for something he believed was right. I was a coward. After all the abuse I'd received inside the same building during my childhood, I hadn't been toughened up enough to defend this poor guy.

My father words of advice rose in my head, "Son, help and protect people. Be a hero, but do not be a stupid hero. If any of the good you are trying to do will claim your life, you need to wait for another opportunity."

I could have rebelled against the guys in uniform, but I knew what would have happened. I needed to wait for another opportunity. I rushed to the barbershop, and I told Rami everything I'd witnessed, leaving out my own desire to select "no" on my ballot.

"He was stupid," Rami said.

I was surprised. "That's your reaction? He is stupid?"

"What do you want me to do? Everyone should know better. Stay far away from such conflicts."

I couldn't rest. I needed to do something. "I'm calling Sam," I told Rami.

"For what? Are you out of your mind? He can't do anything. You'll only get him in trouble too," Rami warned me.

But I ignored him. I called Sam and invited him and Rana over to the house that night, and he agreed. I waited patiently until Sam and Rana walked in.

As soon as we finished greeting each other, I said, "Do you know anything about the guy who voted no?"

Sam said, "Wait, which one? They were serval people today."

"At the School of Khalid Bin Alwaleed—"

Before I finished, he interrupted me, "Oh, that guy." Sam's expression was annoyed.

"Yes, how can we help him?"

Sam hesitated to answer me. Instead, he asked, "Did you know him?"

"No, but I believe what happened to him was unfair. We need to help him."

"It's too late, Adam," Sam replied with a calm tone.

"Why is it too late?" I was stressed. I couldn't believe Sam. He was acting the same way Rami had, as if what had happened was normal, as if it had been the guy's own fault.

"It's too late because he died. He had a heart attack," Sam said flatly.

"What? A heart attack? He was my age for God's sake! They killed him!" I shouted.

I was so defeated. We'd all failed him, including me. And it was personal to me. I might never have met the guy, but we'd had the same desire to vote NO. The only difference between him and me was that I'd been lucky enough to be interrupted by Rana. It was clear to me now that I was living in a country where my life was only one checkmark away from death. I had failed to protect an innocent person today. Instead, I'd decided to wait for the right moment, had decided to be the smart hero my father wanted me to be. But there had been no time for the right moment—the young man was gone!

"You couldn't have done anything, Adam. You did

the right thing by minding your own business. In fact, you protected your family by not doing anything," Sam told me.

My mom, with a worried tone, added, "Adam, this is not over. Life is still ahead of us. One day, you will tell his story. It will be a lesson to all who hear it, and it will expose what the word "dictator" really means. One day, his story could save lives."

"Smart heroes wait for the right moment," I said with a defeated voice.

"Yes, smart heroes wait for the right moment," my mom repeated.

Jon: Today, as I'm writing this book for you, I'm not a hero, but this is the right moment to pay my respects to the guy who said no to dictatorship. 99.96% of people in Iraq, including myself, cowardly voted in favor of our dictator, fearing death. After the national TV announced the 99.96% positive vote, we were officially the joke of the world. But I want you to smile. This was not the worst thing that ever happened to me.

CHAPTER
Twenty

Harsh Letter

Baghdad, 2002
Adam: eighteen years old

My heart was still hurting from the voting crisis. I would never get over it fully, but all my inner demons came lose when I came home one day and saw my mom crying as she read a letter she'd received from my dad and sister in the United States. The letter read as follows:

I am no longer capable of not seeing my family. I've decided I will return and be with my kids. I'm sorry I have failed you. I could not be what you wanted me to be. I miss you and the kids too much. I can no longer continue this expatriation.

My mom wiped her tears with her sleeve. "How can I tell him no?"

"You won't have to—I will," I responded, all the anger in the world pent up inside me. I missed him, but I was convinced we had no future in this country.

"What do you mean?" she asked.

"I will write a letter. I will remind him of what we are going through, don't worry. I will use code words, so we don't get in any trouble."

I went I grabbed peace a paper and started writing. I can't recall every word I wrote, but it was a total of three pages. When my dad read it, he ended up in a hospital. All the anger and pain I had locked away after what I'd witnessed on the day of the vote, I passed to him. The guilt and shame of what I hadn't done fueled my rage, fueled my anger towards him, but it worked. My dad didn't want to talk to us for a few months, but he decided to stay and continue the plan for us all to move there.

All my siblings disapproved of my letter, and Lena told my mom, "Only a person with a cold heart could have written such a letter to his own dad."

But at the time, I needed to punish my dad for not taking every opportunity seriously. This was a matter of life and death, and I was old enough to lead him and my siblings in the right direction.

I sent an apology letter to him later.

Dad,

Sorry for the letter I sent you. But you asked me before you left to take care of my sisters and brother, and here I am, keeping my promise. I did what you asked me. I will continue to say and do what is right to protect them.

—Adam

Jon: I know you think I was a jerk, but smile, this was not the worst thing that ever happened to me.

CHAPTER
Twenty-one

Goodbye for Now

Baghdad, 2003
Adam: nineteen years old

It was after midnight this time when our home phone rang. I woke up, but my mom rushed for the phone, as usual, before I'd even gotten out of bed.

"Hello, Lena?" My mom answered the phone, almost sure it was Lena on the other end.

"It's me." It was my dad, his excited voice loud enough for me to hear through the phone's speaker. "I'm sorry I know it's late, but I couldn't wait until morning to tell you!"

My mom's sleepy eyes were suddenly wide open. "It's all right. What's going on?"

"The application Lena submitted has been approved

for Adam and Rami, since they are under the age of twenty-one. They can come and wait here with me. You can also join us, since your application has been completed."

"Wait. Are you serious? Do you mean now?" My mom couldn't believe it.

"Yes, anytime. I am holding your paperwork and theirs as we speak."

"This is amazing news, but what about Reem?" my mom asked.

Rana was married, and Nabeel and Amar were already finding their way on their own in the world. But Reem...

"She's over the age of twenty-one, so she will have to wait two more years like Nabeel and Rana, a total of ten years since the initial application. But we will do all we can to speed up the process."

My father wanted to comfort my mom, to give her hope, but there was no such thing as speeding up the process. This was the law in the United States—in order to receive visas for your siblings, you had to wait ten years for their applications to process. We were all awake at this point, listening to my dad's booming voice on the other end of the phone. When

I glanced at Reem, she was motionless. If she was upset, she was doing her best not to show it—she said nothing.

My father went on, "So, here is what I think we should do. You and Rami should come over first, since I can only afford two flights anyway, and Adam will stay with Reem and Rana until we have enough money."

I yelled, "No, I'm not staying here, and Reem shouldn't either! She should go stay with Nabeel in Jordan."

My mom gestured for me to be quiet, reminding me that the conversation could be being monitored.

My dad asked my mom, "Is that Adam?"

"Yes, it's him. I think you have an idea what his reaction was."

"Yes, I expected his reaction. Let's talk tomorrow. We will come up with something, I'm sure. I love you all."

As soon as my dad hung up, I told my mom again, "Reem and I are *not* staying behind. I want you to understand that if you and Rami leave, I will go up north. I'll immigrate by walking all the way to Turkey if I have to."

"We will figure something out," my mom said. "I'm also worried about Rana and her kids. How I can leave them here?"

Reem responded, her face emotionless, "Don't worry about me. I will be fine with Rana and the kids. Make sure Adam doesn't stay behind, especially if his visa documents are ready to proceed."

My heart twisted in my chest for Reem. She wasn't showing any emotions, but I knew she was broken-hearted that we were considering leaving her behind. I was powerless. There was nothing I could do to change anything. My only consolation was that if I were in a better place, I would, at least, be able to support her financially.

The next day my dad called and told my mom, "The only way to make this happen is to sell the bar-bershop. But you need to understand, after we sell the barbershop, the only immediate source of income for the family will be myself and Lena. Are you in agree-ment? Should we proceed this way?"

My mom replied with a firm tone, "We need to take the risk. It will be fine."

"Okay, I will send Rami the procuration document, so he can sell the shop." My dad's tone was defeated.

The shop meant a lot to him. He'd had the shop since before any of us were born, so giving it up was like giving up one of his kids.

"Okay, take care of yourself, and don't worry. Everything will be fine." My mom hung up the phone.

I was relieved that he'd come up with a solution that didn't mean leaving me behind. I'd finally leave Iraq for the first time in my life. I'd seen the outside world on my own, not just through movies. I'd have endless opportunities. Selfishly, all my thoughts were about leaving Iraq ... the possibilities. But I also knew I had a clear mission once I left—to support my siblings and friends.

The tensions between the Iraqi government and the United Stated had raised again in 2001 after the 9/11 attack on the World Trade Center had taken place. The news channels were already going on about the war we were about to march into, but this time, they said, it would be the final war. It didn't sound good. We were running out of time, but we had a plan. Rami, Mom, and I would leave during winter break, when we could get a fifteen day's allowance to travel to Jordan—only Jordan. Then, we would proceed with the visas to join my dad.

I'd already started neglecting school. My focus was on receiving a passport and spreading the word about the sale of the shop in the hopes of finding a buyer.

Within a week, Rami found a buyer for the shop. The offer was not great, but it was enough to cover the extra plane ticket, with some leftover to help cover expenses for Rana and Reem for at least a few months.

Rami signed the final papers, and the shop was sold. We were ready to give it away, regardless of all the good and bad memories associated with the place. My father had been working in the same shop since 1979. With him being away, it was the only real chance we had to sell it, because if he were there, I didn't know if he would have been able to let it go.

He knew it too. "I never would have had the strength to sell it myself," he commented when we told him we had finalized the documents.

Rami was sad after we'd finished signing and had received our money. As we got closer to the house, he finally broke his silence. "So, this is it, huh?"

"Yes, this is it, brother," I replied. "We should never be attached to things., and we shouldn't feel bad about letting it go. It's only a place, and we are the ones who create the memories." I'd inherited these words from my dad.

I didn't think Rami agreed with what I'd said, but he told me unexpectedly, "Yes, in this country, we should never be attached to things *or people*, since we could lose anything or anyone at any moment. We have to be prepared."

"Is it even possible not to get attached to the people you love?" I asked him.

"I would say it's not easy, but it is possible. If you are not prepared to lose everything and everyone, you won't be a happy person, Adam." His face was sad as he told me this.

I rejected his words, though I said nothing. I would never be able to detach myself from the people I loved: Mom, Dad, Lena, Rana, Nabeel, Amar, Reem, Rami, my nieces and nephews, you and James. No country or people or land—no reality, no matter how harsh—would force me to prepare myself to lose any of them. It was impossible. They weren't just other people; they were parts of my soul. And for that reason, their love would be part of me forever.

Within days of the shop deal, we were forced to give a big portion of the money to Sam, so that he could bribe the officers responsible for issuing our passports.

But sure enough, within a few days, Sam called home, "The passports are ready, but you must personally pick them up."

Normally, we would have had a short interview with the officers, where they would have asked us a few questions, but since we'd bribed them, no questions were necessary.

"Adam," one of the officers called my first name, not even bothering to say my last name.

I walked toward him to claim my passport, and I asked him while he was handing me my passport, "Do you have Rami's too?"

"Yes, I do," the bribed-officer responded, giving me special treatment. "Where is he?"

"Rami," I called my brother, waving my hand for him to come over.

"Okay, here you go. Enjoy your life." The officer smirked as he gave us the passports, knowing we might never return.

Rami told me, "Open it and make sure it has the correct birth date and name."

I opened my passport. "Oh my God! No!"

Rami asked me. "What? What's wrong?"

"My name is written correctly in Arabic, but it's translated incorrectly in English." I showed Rami what I meant.

"It's written Adem instead of Adam. Do you see what I mean?"

Rami stared at me, annoyed. "Really, Adam, you just freaked me out! Who cares what they'll call you in the US? It doesn't matter as long we get to leave! Your name's spelling in English is the last thing you should worry about!"

My English teacher, Mr.Hani, would not have approved of this translation, but Rami was right. I didn't have the luxury of time to resolve it, and it was the last thing I should have been worrying about. It wouldn't be wise to return to the officers, so they could fix my name in English, and we'd run out of time before they could of fix it anyway.

They'd butchered the translation of name, yet I was still thrilled to receive my passport. I was ready to move to the next step, which was renting a car and driver to take me, Mom, and Rami into Jordan. There were no flights out of Iraq. The only way of travel was by land.

On Friday, the first day of winter break holiday, we

were set to leave, and it was time to say goodbye to more people I deeply loved: Reem, Rana and her two gorgeous kids, and my soulmate friends—you and James. I held it together until the car arrived to pick us up. I told everyone I'd see them soon instead of saying goodbye.

Reem, Rana, and my mom hugged each other for at least ten minutes.

"Let's get going, Mom," I said. "You're not making it any easier on them."

Reem and Rana turned toward me, but I refused to let our goodbye turn into a ten-minute-long, sobbing, hug. Rather, I kissed them on their cheeks, and I promised them we'd see each other again. But as I walked outside, my nephew Fares, who was a little more than two years old now, ran to me, asking for a hug, and that undid me—my heart breaking into tiny pieces. I carried him, hugging him tighter than usual, and began to sob. I couldn't fake strength anymore.

I kissed his cheeks. "I love you so much. I love you so much. I promise we will see each other again." I talked to him as if he were an adult, as if he could understand what I was saying.

My mom said, "It's time, Adam, let's go."

You and James took Fares from me, and you both were crying too. But they couldn't pretend that this was a normal, and they knew they wouldn't see me again soon. They knew this was a goodbye, likely forever. I had a chance to see my family again, but as for seeing my friends again, the likelihood was next to none.

I hugged everyone again and again on my way downstairs.

James said, "At least you don't have climb these stairs anymore, jerk!"

I smiled, and I continued my walk to the SUV. Before I entered the car, I told you and James, "After this, I want you guys to go to the indoor pool and eat dinner from the expensive restaurant." We used to go there every time we felt the world collapsing in on us with pain. I added with a forced smile, tears still on my cheeks, "You will go, and you will have fun. No fucking drama. I need you both to promise me."

They smiled slightly. "Will do. We promise."

Nena yelled from the balcony, "Bye, Nana. Bye, Adam. Bye, Rami." She waived with her tiny arms, smiling, not understanding that we might never see each other again.

I waved back, and so did my mom and Rami next

to me, all three of us sobbing.

I held my mom's hand. "It's okay, Mom." Then, I told the driver, "Let's go. Let's go."

I faced the back-seat window, staring at the apartment where I'd spent so many years suffering, staring as it faded away, getting smaller and smaller, until we made a left turn, and it disappeared.

Rami asked me in Aramaic, "Would you ever go back?"

I answered him in Aramaic, tears already dry on my cheeks, "On one condition, if the people of Iraq built, by the city's entrance, a Masjid, a church, and a synagogue—a temple for every religion in the world, a symbol acceptance for everyone—then I would go back. No, I have more conditions. If the people of Iraq accepted others regardless of how they speak, regardless whether they have perfect or broken accents. If the people of Iraq accepted everyone regardless of a person's appearance—white, black, or tan—regardless of a person's sexual orientation—straight or gay. When acceptance for all is achieved, then I would step foot in this city again."

Rami, with a defeated tone, replied, "In other words, your answer is never."

I gazed through the side window to the clear sky of Baghdad while replying to Rami, "If it's never, then here I am, saying goodbye to the city."

Jon: I want you to smile, living in Iraq was not the worst thing that ever happened to me.

CHAPTER
Twenty-two

Loneliness

Fremont, California 2017
Adam: thirty-three years old

"So, what is it?" Jon asks. "What's the worst thing that ever happened to you? You never say, even though that's what I requested."

"You read everything?" I ask him.

"Yes. But you didn't answer my question," he says, determined to find out.

"I am coming back to Michigan. I quit my job. I will be there on Wednesday. I will tell you in person what the worst thing was."

"Wait, you quit your job?" He sounds surprised. "Does your family know you are going back?"

"Yes, I did, and they do. I'm not happy here. I miss

my family and you too, jerk."

"That's great," Jon says. "But I won't wait until Wednesday to find out. You should know me better than that."

I try to change the subject. "Has James called you recently?"

"No, he hasn't," he answers and then adds, "Was it the company you work for? Were you going to kill yourself over work?"

"No," I respond.

"Was it Pauleen? I thought you guys agreed to only one hookup, and that was it."

"No, it wasn't Pauleen." I sigh. Pauleen and I were "friends with benefits" when I was living in Michigan back in 2010.

He sounds certain of himself when he says, "Shit, I knew Sara would fuck with your mind."

"No, it wasn't Sara. Are you just going to list all the girls I've ever slept with? None of them matter to me—it was only sex."

I add, "Well, let me ask you this, Jon?"

"Go ahead. I'm listening."

"When we were living in Iraq, what kept us going?" I ask him.

"I don't know ... hope?"

"Be more specific. What specifically keeps you going?"

After a few seconds of silence, he answers, "My family and my friends."

I answer with a sad tone. "True, and I've lost them both here. It didn't matter how bad our situation was, because we all had each other to comfort and uplift our spirits. Today, I'm living here in Fremont alone, and all my siblings are married and living all over the world. James is living in Las Vegas, and I talk to you over the phone daily, but sometimes, when I don't see you in person, I wonder if you're real or just part of my imagination."

"That's life, Adam" Jon responds.

"I know. That loneliness is why I thought of ending it—"

Before I finish what I want to say, he hangs up.

"Hello, Jon." I glance at my phone screen, and it's a black screen, as if I'd never opened it. *Maybe it died.* I think to myself.

I finish packing my luggage, and I wait patiently for Wednesday to come, so I can go back to Michigan, to the place I now think of as home, where my mom and my father live.

In the morning, I finally arrive at the Detroit Airport, but Jon is nowhere to be found. I wonder if he is mad at me for what I told him earlier, wonder if he thinks I wasted his time. I want to apologize, so I call him, but he doesn't answer. I leave him a voicemail, telling him I am taking an uber home, and I will be expecting him at my parent's house for dinner.

As soon as I arrive home, my mom is waiting on the porch, and she hugs me and kisses me countless times.

"Okay, Mom, stop it. You know I'm not a hugger."

We laugh and go inside the house.

My father is sitting in the living room waiting. He tries to get up, but his age betrays him—he can barely walk. I rush to him, and I kiss him.

My mom has already prepared dinner—they were waiting for me.

"Let's eat, son," my mom says in an excited tone, always happy when she gets to feed my endless appetite.

"Mom, let's wait for Jon. I'm not sure why he didn't pick me up from the airport, but I'm sure he will call me back."

My mom freezes, and all her earlier excitement changes to worry.

"What is wrong, Mom? Is he okay?" I ask her.

I hold her hand when she starts crying.

"Adam, are you still taking your medication?" she asks me, with tears in her eyes and pity on her face.

"What? Are you okay? Mom, you're scaring me."

"Son, Jon died back in 2003 when the United States army invaded Iraq to take out Saddam Hussein. He was shot and killed by the radicals. Don't you remember? I've told you countless times, but you always forget."

She hugs me, and my mind goes blank for a few seconds. I try to recall everything, and suddenly, like a puzzle board, all the pieces start fitting together until the whole picture is revealed in my mind.

"Jon was never there," I say. "Jon is dead. Yes, I remember they showed me the video of his death. They shot him in the head, and his brain spilled all over the cement floor." I ask my mom, "Do you know ... did anyone clean his blood from the floor? Did they bury him? Is his family still alive?"

She responds, but I don't really want to listen to any of her answers. I rush to the book I wrote at Jon's request, or the book I *thought* I wrote at Jon's request, and I write down a final sentence before I forget it again. I can't keep my hands steady—they are trembling as I write, and forehead sweat is dripping on the paper along with my tears—but I continue writing my final sentence.

Jon ... Jon ... Jon ...

I write his name a hundred times, and then I add ...

It was you—*it was you all along. You created the loneliness in my soul. Losing you, my best friend, was the worst thing that ever happened to me.*